MORFORWYN

MORFORWYN

MERYL E. HODGSON

ILLUSTRATIONS BY M. BAGNULO

authorHOUSE®

AuthorHouse™ UK Ltd.
1663 Liberty Drive
Bloomington, IN 47403 USA
www.authorhouse.co.uk
Phone: 0800.197.4150

Published by AuthorHouse   07/18/2013

ISBN: 978-1-4817-7034-7 (sc)
ISBN: 978-1-4817-7035-4 (e)

With my heartfelt thanks to Steve
for all his encouragement and enthusiasm for this book
and
for Ayla, my true inspiration.
This is for you

Morforwyn *Welsh n. the mermaid (Mor-VOR-win)*

CHAPTER 1

This wasn't the holiday Bindy wanted. Nearly all her friends at school had either been to amazing, exotic places or were planning to go to Disneyland, Florida to see all those amazing characters she'd watched since she was a little girl. All her favourites like Aurora, Belle and Ariel, but here she was in Wales stuck on a hill in an old holiday cottage with Mum, Dad and the dog. What sort of fun was that?

She rested her head in her hands while she sat on a sofa by the window recovering from the long, tiring journey and looked down at the other cottages nestling on the hillside each side of the sandy path which led down to the beach. They were all painted in pastel colours—pink, blue, lemon, green, and lilac. If her parents had chosen the pink one, at least she could have pretended she was living in a princess's cottage, but white! *Ugh!* Boring! Who'd want to stay in a cottage that's white when it could be any colour of the rainbow? The only nice thing about it was that it was called Pearl Cottage because she really liked pearls.

She rose from the chair and walked to the mirror above the fireplace to gaze at her reflection. She ran her fingers through her dark blond hair which had been very long a few weeks ago. It was now falling to her shoulders and she still wished she hadn't had it cut. She fluffed it up a bit and sighed then turning away from the mirror she went back to the window. As she gazed out and brooded over her misfortunes she saw the grey clouds overhead and decided to go out into the garden before the rain came. She put on her sandals, straightened her t-shirt over her jeans and walked through the small house to the kitchen door. Trilby, their liver and white Springer spaniel, looked up and wagged his tail hopefully at Bindy.

'Come on, then.' Bindy said and opened the door for them both to go out and explore.

The garden wasn't very big but it had a lovely cherry blossom tree and all the petals had fallen on the grass making it look like pink snow. Around the trunk of the tree was a seat where Bindy thought she might enjoy reading. She was an avid reader and most of all loved to read about the sea and creatures real and mythical that make their homes there. Whenever she had a wish she always wished to be a mermaid because she thought they were so beautiful with their long hair and elegant tails swishing in the water.

Trilby darted out of the door and sniffed frantically around the garden. He seemed very interested in something and started scratching at the grass. Bindy walked over to see what it was. It was just an old rusty ring attached to a flat stone buried in the longer grass at the edge of the garden. It had been there for years and years by the look of it. Bindy pulled at it to see if it would move but it was firmly stuck and nothing was going to move it.

'You won't shift it.' shouted a voice. Bindy spun around in surprise and saw a girl, a bit older than herself, peering over the fence licking an iced lolly. She had two long, wavy bunches of dark reddish-brown hair and had a pretty face with freckles on her nose and cheeks. She wore a pink striped T-shirt and cropped jeans. The girl took another great lick of her lolly and continued, 'We've got one just like it in our garden. Dad tried to move it but he reckons it's something to do with the drains.'

'Oh.' said Bindy, a bit at a loss as to what else to say.

'By the way, my name's Cassie, short for Cassandra, and we're staying in Musselshell Cottage, over there.' She pointed to a blue cottage two doors higher up on the opposite side of the lane from Bindy's. 'We've been here two days and you're the only other girl here, the rest are babies and older boys. What's your name?'

Bindy walked closer to Cassie and said, 'I'm Bindy and this is Trilby.'

Cassie opened the gate, walked into the garden and bent down to make a fuss of Trilby, who wagged his tail madly at the new visitor.

'I like dogs, but Mum says they're too much work, we've got cats. What's Bindy short for?'

'Belinda, but I hate being called that. Have you got your cats with you?'

'Yes, Mum says we're never going to put them in a cattery ever again!'

'Why is that?' asked Bindy.

'Because last time they pined for us so much, they stopped eating, the silly things, so we have to bring them with us. Would you like to see them?'

'Oh, yes, please." Bindy exclaimed, "Come on, we'll take Trilby back inside and we can ask my mum if it's OK.'

Eagerly, she opened the door and they all trooped inside. Bindy introduced Cassie to her mum who was in the kitchen unpacking the things they'd brought. They chatted for a little while then Bindy asked if it was alright if she went over to Cassie's to see the cats.

'OK, but don't be too long because I'll be making some food for us soon. Cassie, you're welcome to join us if you like, it's only something simple.'

'OK, thanks, I'll ask my mum.' Cassie replied happily.

The girls walked up the stony sandy lane to Musselshell Cottage picking some of the pretty wild flowers growing in the hedgerows. Bindy learnt that Cassie's second name was Barton, she was eleven years old and her birthday was in April, she liked dancing, singing, and collecting things. When Bindy asked what kind of things she collected, Cassie just said, 'anything that looks pretty'. She had shells, jewellery, hair slides, pebbles and other things that she kept in her own private treasure box. Bindy thought this sounded wonderful and that she'd like a treasure box too.

When they arrived at the cottage, Cassie's parents were sitting in the garden enjoying a drink. When they heard the girls' voices they turned towards them with a smile as they walked through the gate. Mr Barton was tall and lanky and wore glasses and Mrs Barton had short red hair with lots of curls. Cassie handed the small bunch of flowers to her Mum.

'Oh, they're lovely, Cassie, and I see you've found a friend. What's your name, sweetheart?'

'Belinda, but everyone calls me Bindy.'

'You're not Windy Bindy, are you!' laughed Mr Barton.

'*DAD!*' shouted Cassie, 'Why do you always have to embarrass everyone! Bindy, please excuse him; he's the most awful father sometimes. He thinks he's *so* funny but as you can tell he's just plain impossible! Anyway, follow me and you can meet the cats.' She glared one more time at her father and took Bindy into the house.

In the lounge were two beautiful cream Siamese cats, one with brown ears, paws and tail and the other sand coloured. They were curled up together looking very sleepy in their cat bed. Cassie and Bindy knelt down beside them.

'They're brother and sister.' Cassie explained, 'His name's Simba,' she said, pointing to the chocolate coloured one, 'and she's Sandy Claws. That's my father being funny again, get it? Sandy Claws—Santa Claus, because we had them at Christmas time! We call her Sandy.' Bindy grinned at the joke and then looked back at the cats.

'They're so beautiful.' breathed Bindy, never having seen Siamese cats before, 'We'll have to keep Trilby away from them, I don't think he likes cats. Anyway, go and ask your Mum if you can come over for supper.' They went back into the garden and Cassie asked Mrs Barton if it was alright for her to join Bindy for something to eat. Mrs Barton said it was OK but for Cassie to be home by 7.30 so off they went back to Pearl Cottage. As they wandered back down the lane they began to chat away together as if they'd known each other for ever, and Bindy began to think that this holiday might not be so bad after all.

CHAPTER 2

The following morning, Bindy blinked sleepily around the strange room and remembered where she was. She jumped out of bed to see what the weather was like. Overhead the white fluffy clouds moved gently against a large area of blue and the sun was shining on the garden making the tree and seat look very inviting indeed.

She went through the tiny cottage to her parents' room. They were still sleeping so she tiptoed out to the kitchen and opened the fridge. Trilby's wet nose felt cold against her leg as he tried to push his nose into the fridge to catch the scent of something tasty.

'Stop that, Trilby, I'll give you some food in a minute.' She got out some milk, poured herself a glass and sat by the lounge window which overlooked the sea. It looked fabulous, a wonderful bright blue-green colour, and the seagulls were calling overhead. She wondered whether Cassie would come for a walk with her to the beach after breakfast and decided that she'd get dressed, get her parents up and ask them.

Later, while they were all sitting at the breakfast table finishing their toast, Bindy asked,

'Dad, would it be alright if I asked Cassie to come for a walk on the beach this morning? I'll take Trilby so that he can have a run around too and we'll be ever so careful, I promise. Can we?' She crossed the fingers of both hands under the table and looked at her parents with big pleading eyes. Her Dad smiled broadly and after glancing at her Mum said,

'I think that would be a very good idea, Bindy. In fact, Mum and I were going to have a walk down there ourselves later, so how would it be if we joined you both with a picnic, say about twelve?'

'Oh, great! Thanks!' She got up, gave him a hug, and then dashed towards the door.

'I'll go and ask her straight away, then come back for Trilby if she says yes.' Bindy loved the idea of going to the beach; she may find all sorts of lovely things to collect, just like Cassie, and start off her own box of treasures.

When she arrived at Cassie's cottage they were all inside clearing up their breakfast dishes.

'Hello, Windy Bindy, how are you this bright, sunny morning?' smiled Mr Barton. His wife gave him a friendly thump and smiled at Bindy.

'Ignore him, Bindy,' she advised, 'Are you and your parents settled into your cottage now?'

'Yes, thanks. We're going to have a picnic on the beach this afternoon, so would it be alright if Cassie came down for a walk with me and Trilby now and then my parents will meet us there later?' She turned and smiled at Cassie. 'Could she, please?'

Cassie's face lit up in a big smile 'I'd really like that, Mum. Can I go?'

'Well OK, Cassie, but make sure you wear your trainers as the walk down there is quite rocky, and take some sun lotion in your rucksack and your waterproofs too in case it starts to rain'

'The sun's shining, Mum!'

'You never know, it might rain.'

Cassie rolled her eyes at Bindy, but gave her the thumbs up sign and said,

'I'll get my stuff ready and meet you at your place as soon as I can, but hang on, before you go, I want to show you something.' She took Bindy's hand and pulled her towards the garden.

'Remember that drain cover with the ring attached that we both have in our gardens?' Bindy nodded. 'Well, I looked at ours again last night and started to push some of the overgrown grass away from the edges and it's got some funny shape carved into it. Look.' She pointed at the stone which was now quite large and at its centre, near the metal ring, was a deep carving of something curved. Around the edge, previously hidden by the grass, was some writing. Peering closer, Bindy read out loud,

"Find the key, turn the bone and speak the name that lifts the stone.' Gosh!' whispered Bindy 'Have you shown anyone else?'

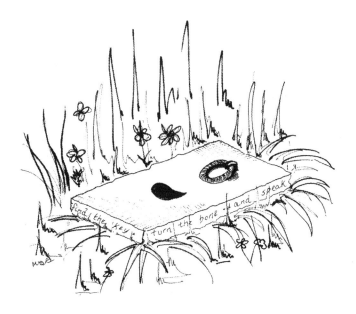

Cassie shook her head. 'I thought we could make it our holiday secret, and have a treasure hunt, what do you think?'

'Oh, yeah!' answered Bindy with a grin. Then she thought about the one in *her* garden. They must have been thinking the same thing as they both looked at each other and said,

'Let's check the one in Pearl cottage!'

'OK,' Cassie said, 'but don't look till I get there. See you in a few minutes!' and ran inside to get herself ready for the beach.

In a quarter of an hour Bindy had Trilby on a lead, a bottle of water for him in her rucksack together with an apple and a drink for herself. She had trainers on and shorts and a T-shirt, with her jacket wrapped around her waist. While she walked towards the stone Cassie came dashing through the gate to meet her.

'Well, have you checked?'

'No' said Bindy 'I said I'd wait for you. Come on!'

They knelt down in the grass and pushed away all the overgrown weeds and tall grasses. They turned to each other in surprise, for there carved in exactly the same position as the one in Cassie's, was another symbol. This time it was a plain shape, as if a ball had been pressed into it but the rhyme was the same.

'*Find the key, turn the bone and speak the name that lifts the stone.*'

The girls began to giggle excitedly, they couldn't believe their eyes.

'Crumbs, I wonder if all the cottages have one of these. What do you think it means?' asked Bindy. 'If these stones move, what's in there?' She paused. 'Do you think they lead anywhere?' They both thought about this.

'Maybe they don't *lead* anywhere,' replied Cassie, 'but perhaps they store things . . . .' A gleam came into her eyes, ' . . . . like pirate treasure . . . or . . . . or maybe it's just nothing at all, a big hole.' She sighed, sad at the thought that it might all be a waste of time.

'Well, whatever it is,' said Bindy, 'let's go and do some searching for two things that fit these shapes.

'But they could be anywhere! What sort of things would fit those shapes? I mean, ones washed up on the beach aren't going to be the right things, are they?'

'Perhaps they're made of bone!' suggested Bindy, thinking of the rhyme.

They wandered around the edges of the garden and path looking for something that might suit. Then they checked the shape in the stone again. It had, in the centre, a deep slit, which meant that the object also had a bit sticking out at the back of it which had to fit down into the hole, and it had to be quite a hard object, otherwise it wouldn't stay in place. The girls looked at each other with puzzled expressions. Trilby whined and pulled hard at his lead, he was getting fed up of waiting for his walk on such a lovely day.

'Come on, Cassie, let's go, Trilby's getting impatient.' She gave him a loving pat as they began their walk.

The girls decided that while they were on the beach, they may as well start looking for these mystery objects, maybe something would turn up. As they walked on, the sun glistened on the sea and made them feel rather excited.

CHAPTER 3

As the girls passed each cottage on the way down to the beach, they couldn't help looking into the gardens to see if they could spot any other stones hidden away in dark corners. They thought they saw one but decided that for now they'd concentrate on looking for the objects on the beach.

When they got there, Bindy unclipped Trilby's lead and he ran down the dunes with his tail wagging furiously. Glad to be free to run around and sniff at all the new smells, he was in dog heaven!

Being early summer, and not particularly warm, there were only a few other people on the beach; some walking their dogs, others playing or sitting on the sand. Trilby lost no opportunity in making friends with all the other four-legged creatures he could spot and scampered around happily. The golden beach looked wonderful, with its cliffs, caves and rock pools. The girls ran down the dunes and decided to scout around in search of their mystery objects.

After much searching they began to feel tired and a bit disappointed that they hadn't found anything suitable. They thought it would be a good idea to sit down, have a snack, and think of some better ideas. Looking across the beach, they decided to climb up to the highest rocks so that they could have a good view across the whole beach. They gave Trilby some water and told him to 'stay' while they began to negotiate the rocks.

As they climbed higher, they seemed to think that one of the big rocks above them might be a cave where they could sit and enjoy their snack. When they eventually arrived at its mouth, they were quite startled to see a young girl at the entrance, almost hidden behind other rocks. She was busy doing something with seaweed, although what it was, they couldn't quite tell.

'Oh, I'm sorry!' Bindy, exclaimed, 'We didn't know anyone was here.

The girl looked up slowly. It was difficult to guess her age, probably about seventeen. She had long wavy fair hair that fell down to her waist. Her eyes were an intense green and she held their gaze for a few moments before answering.

'You're welcome to sit awhile.' Her voice was soft and musical. She didn't smile but her face gave them a gentle and kind look. She was kneeling down and her lap was covered with a blanket of intertwined multicoloured seaweeds. She bent her head once more to carry on with her task of attaching shells of all sizes and colours to the seaweed blanket. Although very aware of this girl, Bindy and Cassie took out their apples and enjoyed a long thirst-quenching drink. Bindy checked on Trilby who was still lying where they'd left him gnawing at a bit of driftwood.

'May we ask what you're making?' Cassie asked the girl.

The girl raised her head again very slowly and fixed them with her piercing gaze. 'You may ask, but I cannot tell.'

Cassie and Bindy looked at each other with raised eyebrows. The girl returned to her work. Intrigued, Bindy tried another question. 'Are you on holiday like us or do you live round here?' Again, she stopped her work and looked at them, watching them carefully.

'My home is what you see.'

There was a long pause. The girls shared a silent giggle together and whispered *weird* as they watched her fingers move nimbly, threading more shells onto the seaweed.

15

Good sense would have made them retreat and avoid any further discussion but, spurred on by curiosity, Cassie said,

'We're staying in the cottages on the hill over there,' she pointed to their holiday homes, 'and we're on an adventure.'

'Yes.' Bindy continued 'Do you know anything about them?'

The girl smiled. 'Of course.' she replied and paused for a little while then said, 'I watch them during sunlight hours and wait.'

'What do you wait for?' asked the girls together, now very intrigued by this person.

'I wait for . . . . my destiny to change.'

Although they were beginning to realise that this girl was really peculiar, neither Bindy nor Cassie made any move to leave. It was as if they were getting drawn deeper into another mystery, a mystery about this girl, although everything she said didn't make much sense. What was going on here?

Cassie decided to tell her about their adventures. She began by explaining to her that they had discovered mysterious stones in their cottage gardens. As soon as the girl heard this she laid down her work and stared at them intently. She didn't utter a word but waited quietly, almost holding her breath. Bindy watched her reaction—this girl was now very interested in what they had to say.

Cassie was coming to the end of the story,

' . . . and so that's why we're here at the beach looking hard for the two shapes, but so far we've not found anything. That's why we came up here to have a rest and look across the beach to see if we could get any more ideas. We're a bit stuck, any suggestions?'

The girl turned away from them and gazed out to sea looking puzzled and thoughtful. After a while she turned back and looked at them, her face sweet and gentle, giving them a lovely smile.

'Your search down here is of no use. Return to all the cottages on the hill and you'll find the answers at each one. I cannot tell you any more. You must go now.'

'But . . . where at the cottages?' Cassie asked. 'There's nothing inside them, they're cleared for each visitor.'

'Just use your eyes carefully, look at everything and soon all will be clear. Now go and don't share your secret but be steadfast and fearless and you shall be rewarded.'

'Can we come and tell you when we've found the answer, please?' asked Cassie who found this person most captivating.

'Oh yes, you must!' The girl looked at them with intensity. She bent down and picked out two shiny green shells, the colours within them were beautiful; almost like iridescent glass, shimmering with lots of different colours. She held them out to Bindy and Cassie in the palm of her hand and as they took them, they noticed, with some surprise, that her fingers were webbed.

'If you need to speak to me again, return to this place, hold these shells in the palms of your hands and whisper my name into it.'

'But what *is* your name?' asked Bindy, as they rose to leave.

'Morforwyn' she whispered, as she waved them goodbye.

CHAPTER 4

Bindy and Cassie clambered down from the rocks to join Trilby who, although very happy to see them, ran ahead, proudly carrying his piece of driftwood in his mouth. The girls ran to the top of the beach where they'd agreed to meet Bindy's parents for lunch and flopped side by side on the soft sand. For a while they stared out to sea, neither of them really wanting to break the spell of the moment. After a minute or two, Cassie eventually said,

'Pinch me hard, Bindy, I think I must be dreaming!'

Bindy duly gave her a very hard pinch.

'*Ouch!* You didn't have to pinch me *that* hard!' She rubbed her arm with a look of mock disapproval and confirmed, 'OK, it's real!' They looked at each other and exploded into giggles, partly out of fun and to a certain extent from the thrill of this bizarre experience.

Cassie gazed at the rocks where they'd been but she could see nothing of Morforwyn or the cave.

'Bindy, did you see her webbed fingers? I mean, we weren't imagining things, were we?'

'I can't believe what we just saw,' said Bindy excitedly. 'Do you think she's a mermaid?' She asked this, unsure of whether to believe it or not.

'I don't know, I mean, look at this shell, I've never seen a shell as pretty as this before.'

Bindy agreed and immediately realised that she had her very first 'treasure' to start her collection.

'I mean, where did she get these from? Cassie continued. 'All the ones on the beach are ordinary,' she said, picking some up from the soft sand in front of her, 'look, boring brown and cream ones.'

Bindy looked at them and nodded absently. Looking up, she took a deep breath and let out a big sigh. 'What am I going to tell my parents when they come?'

'Heck, I hadn't thought of that! What *are* we going to do? Do you think we should tell them?'

Bindy pondered the problem. She had always told them everything; all her fears and worries, every little problem she had and they'd always valued her honesty. Lying to them would be awful. Keeping a secret from them would be just as bad. She didn't know what to do. Half of her wanted to share her experience with them and the other half felt loyalty to the beautiful young girl.

'I don't know.' she replied, and felt a bit uncomfortable. She gazed at the shell and it crossed her mind to run back to Morforwyn and call on her for advice on what to do but at that moment she heard a shout behind her.

'Hi you two, lunch has arrived!' It was her Mum and Dad.

She hurriedly put the shell into her pocket and whispered to Cassie, 'Not yet. OK?' Cassie nodded in agreement.

The picnic was delicious. Roast chicken legs, celery sticks, cherry tomatoes, crisps, fresh buttered rolls, with different fillings, juicy, sweet grapes and apples and some snack bars to finish off with a bottle of Cream Soda. Mr. Hammond had also brought down his camera and was taking photographs of the views and of them with full mouths and bulging cheeks. Bindy and Cassie hadn't realized how hungry they were and laughed when he told them they looked like a pair of hamsters.

'Thank you for such a yummy lunch, Mrs. Hammond.' said Cassie.

'You're very welcome.' she replied, 'It's a pleasure to make food for people who are so appreciative. You must have worked up a very good appetite, what have you been doing?'

Bindy gave Cassie a subtle dig with her elbow.

'Oh, we've been walking and climbing . . . . and throwing sticks for Trilby, he's had a great time.'

'Well that's certainly good news,' said Mrs. Hammond, 'the poor thing didn't get much exercise yesterday. So, what are you planning to do for the rest of the day?'

The girls looked at each other then Bindy piped up, 'How about coming back to ours and playing there, I've brought a couple of games with me and there were some in the cupboard when we arrived.'

'Yes, alright,' replied Cassie 'and then you can come over to mine.'

'Well you're pretty well sorted.' said Mr. Hammond, 'Of course, we'll want to go and explore the surroundings tomorrow so make the most of your time together today, because there are lots of places to visit around here.'

'OK, Dad.' smiled Bindy. 'Can we go up to Pearl Cottage now?'

'Yes. Mum and I will follow you up in a minute, once we've tidied the food things away and because you've been such good dog walkers this morning we'll bring Trilby up as well. Here's the key.'

'OK, thanks. See you soon.'

As the girls climbed back up the hill towards the cottage they tried to recall what Morforwyn had said about finding the clues. They remembered she'd said that they would find the answers at each cottage, which meant that they had to search their own and eight others!

They soon arrived back at Pearl Cottage. Cassie thought she'd better let her parents know where she was and also to check if it was OK to go over there later. She returned soon after with a couple of iced lollies her Mum had made. The girls sat under the tree on the seat enjoying the sweet juicy taste and thinking their own special thoughts. Eventually they decided that they'd better start looking inside the cottages for clues. They took out some games, in case their parents checked up on them, and then they started searching. They looked in drawers, on top of cupboards, under beds, everywhere they could possibly think of.

Meanwhile, Mr. and Mrs. Hammond had returned some time ago and were lying in the garden on their sun loungers, reading and listening to the radio. This was good news for the girls as it gave them freedom to search. After an hour and a half they'd been on their knees, on tiptoes, climbing on chairs, lying on the floor, searching above, below, inside, outside and were now exhausted from their fruitless efforts.

'Phew!' cried Bindy, 'this is turning out to be so much harder than I thought.'

'I know,' replied Cassie, 'I'm fed up and tired and need a rest.' She flopped down on the settee and closed her eyes. Bindy went to the fridge to get refreshments while Cassie sat and pondered.

'Don't worry, Cassie,' said Bindy, placing a can and a biscuit in front of her friend, 'Morforwyn said that if we need help we can call on her. Why don't we wait and see what we can find in your cottage first, then, if we still don't find anything, we'll go back to see her?'

'OK, you're probably right.' Cassie agreed as she crunched her biscuit.

It was now half past three. The old clock on the mantelpiece ticked noisily in the silence. Just then they heard new voices in the garden. Bindy glanced out of the window and noticed that Mr. and Mrs. Barton had arrived with a bottle of wine and some glasses. They dashed over to the window and heard them say,

'Hi, we thought as our daughters were so friendly we should come and introduce ourselves and get acquainted too. We brought a bottle of wine with us, if you'd like some?'

'What a lovely idea!' replied Mr. Hammond 'Come and sit down.' They shook hands and he drew out some chairs from the garden shed for them to sit on.

'Well,' smiled Cassie, 'this looks like a party to me!' and the girls giggled as they watched their parents get acquainted.

CHAPTER 5

As the afternoon wore on, the girls' parents really enjoyed their time in the garden but it was soon time for the Bartons to go back to their cottage. This was just what Cassie wanted so she and Bindy followed them over to Musselshell Cottage to do a search there.

Despite their efforts, it became clear that their search at Cassie's cottage was also unproductive. To the girls' dismay, they discovered absolutely nothing. As they wandered around outside in the garden, they searched near the stone once more to see if they had missed anything but all they found was the stone with its carving and the verse.

The door of the cottage was open so Cassie went over to close it so that they could not be overheard by her parents. As she slammed it shut she leaned her back against it and said,

'Maybe we need to go back to see *you-know-who.*'

'*Awww,*' moaned Bindy, 'I felt certain we'd find something. It can't be far away if it's meant to be here somewhere.' She looked up towards the roof. 'It wouldn't be up there, would it?' she asked incredulously.

'I really don't think so and anyway, if it is, *I'm* not going up there, no way!'

Just at that moment the door opened again and Mrs Barton came out with a tray of hot pizza and some drinks for them. She had a rug under her arm.

'Come on, girls, come and sit down here.' She spread the rug onto the lawn and placed the tray on top of it.

'Oh thanks, Mum,' smiled Cassie and soon they forgot their immediate problem as they munched hungrily at their pizza. After they'd eaten they lay down on the rug thinking about their next move, plucking absently at the grass when, all of a sudden, Bindy sat up, and looked up at the cottage her eyes growing like saucers. She cried,

'Oh . . . my . . . *gosh!* Look! I think it's there! It's been staring us in the face all this time!'

'Where?' Cassie cried, jumping up and trying to follow her friend's gaze.

Bindy rose and walked slowly towards the cottage. To the left of the door, slightly higher than their heads, was the name of the cottage on a stone plaque, 'Musselshell Cottage' it read, and underneath was a carved mussel shell standing proud underneath the lettering. The curved shape was just like the one they were looking for! Bindy's hand went to touch it to see if it moved. She curled her small fingers around it and began to pull gently and twist and turn it and then . . . . it happened! The stone mussel shell loosened and came away from the name plate. Bindy's knees began to wobble and she began to quiver all over with excitement. She looked at Cassie with round, staring eyes. Cassie stared back and looked at the mussel shell in disbelief. At the back of it was a strong thick cream coloured stick which was about ten centimetres long and at the end was a key-type shape. Cassie took the carving from Bindy and studied it carefully.

'I need to sit down,' whispered Bindy.

'So do I.' Cassie whispered back and they both began to laugh uncontrollably as they sat on the rug feeling completely triumphant.

'We've done it, I don't believe it! We've found it!' they kept saying over and over to each other with huge smiles of satisfaction.

'So does this mean that all the clues are hidden in the name plates do you think?' Cassie suggested.

'Well, we'd better go and see. What shall we do with this one?'

'We'll put it back' said Cassie 'and decide later on.'

They quickly replaced the mussel shell key and ran down to Pearl Cottage. They looked at the name plate and there, sure enough, was another carving, but of course it was a 'pearl' not a ball!

Bindy's parents were still relaxing in the garden so, while they weren't looking, Bindy did the same wiggling and jiggling to the pearl and felt it loosen under her hand. She nodded to Cassie to show her that it was the same as the mussel shell and they gave each other a big hug and shrieked loudly.

'You two sound as if you're having fun!' shouted her Dad from his lounger, 'What's up?'

'Nothing that dads would find at all amusing.' laughed Bindy as she danced around Cassie.

'Don't be so sure.' her Dad smiled, as he went back to reading his paper.

In her heart Bindy felt guilty that her parents still didn't know what she and Cassie were involved in. Maybe later tonight I'll tell them, she thought. I'll speak to Cassie.

'Come on Cassie, let's go to my room.'

When they got there she confessed how she was feeling to her friend.

'I'm beginning to feel I ought to tell my parents what's going on, what do you think?'

'I know what you mean, but didn't the girl say we were not to tell a soul?'

'That's right, she did. What did she say again? We had to be steadfast and brave or something didn't she? What does steadfast mean?'

'I'm not sure. Why don't you ask your Dad?'

'OK, hold on.' Bindy ran to the window and shouted loudly to her father.'Dad, what does steadfast mean?'

He put his paper down and thought for a moment.

'It means you're firm and committed to something.'

'Thanks.' She closed the window. 'Did you hear that?'

'Yeah,' replied Cassie, 'that means we can't give up until we've solved the mystery. That suits me! If we get stuck or need someone's help, we've got the shells and we can call Morforwyn. Shall we stick with that for now?'

'OK, I suppose you're right.'

'Sure?'

'Yeah.'

'So what shall we do next?'

'I think we need to open the stones to see what's inside. We can't do ours because Dad's in the garden and he'll see us. What about trying yours while your parents are inside the cottage?'

'Good idea.'

The girls headed once again for Musselshell Cottage. As they got there Mrs Barton was leaving with a shopping bag on her arm. A lady, by the name of Mrs Easterson, ran a mobile shop which came to the car park at the top of the hill. It supplied groceries to the holidaymakers three times a week.

'I'm just going to buy a few things from Mrs. Easterson. Your father's indoors watching the snooker' said her mother, 'so don't disturb him, it's the final!'

'Great', thought Cassie, *just what we needed.'*

When her mother had gone, she pulled Bindy towards the door.

'Let's go for it!'

Cassie gently moved the carved shell from the name plate and took it to the stone in the corner of the garden. Once there, they re-read the verse,

'Find the key, turn the bone and speak the name that lifts the stone.'

Cassie placed the 'key' into the centre slit. Gently, she pushed it but it stopped about half way down. She tried wiggling it a bit and then she turned it slowly to the left and felt it slot into a groove. Again, it started to move down further, but because the shape was out of alignment she had to turn it again to the right. It took a little pressure to get it to sit perfectly but eventually it slotted into place perfectly, as if it was one piece of stone. Cassie let out a deep sigh.

'Now what?' she asked Bindy.

'Speak the name that lifts the stone.'

'What's the word?'

'I don't know. Let's try Morforwyn.' Bindy suggested.

Holding the ring tightly, Cassie said in a strong voice, *'Morforwyn!'*

They waited. Nothing.

'What else could it be?' she asked.

'Mermaid?'

Cassie tried again using 'mermaid' but still nothing happened. Bindy looked at Cassie with a disappointed expression.

'I think we need help from Morforwyn!'

CHAPTER 6

T he next day, both families went to visit some local attractions. As each family went their separate ways, the girls didn't see each other until late afternoon.

Bindy and her parents had been to see a few local landmarks, shopped a little at a nearby town and ended the day at a local theme park where they enjoyed themselves on some really scary rides. Meanwhile, Cassie and her family had visited some relatives in the morning who had taken them on to some famous cave formations which Cassie enjoyed, particularly as she kept thinking that Morforwyn would know all about caves and their stalagmites and stalactites.

When they eventually got home, Cassie ran across to Pearl Cottage to see if Bindy would be able to come down to the beach to see Morforwyn. Luckily, they hadn't been home very long and as Trilby needed a long walk, they were allowed to go, as long as they were back for supper at 6 o'clock. That gave them an hour.

They climbed the high rocks and sat outside the cave entrance, both having remembered to bring their special green shells. They held them in their hands and whispered *'Morforwyn'*.

At first, nothing could be heard but then they heard a shuffling sound and Morforwyn appeared at the entrance with her lovely long hair trailing over her shoulders. Today she was wearing what looked like a net headdress encrusted with pearls and so intricately woven it looked like it could belong to a princess. Her body was covered in garments made of pink seaweed and again they shimmered with lovely shells. She was the most amazing image of loveliness. The girls gulped and whispered,

'Hi, Morforwyn.'

She smiled sweetly. 'Have you got some news to tell me?'

'Yes,' they answered together, 'but we're a bit stuck.'

'We found the keys,' Cassie explained, 'and worked out how to open the stones but we don't know the word to use. We tried your name but that didn't work and we also tried . . . .' She stopped abruptly and looked at Bindy, feeling the colour rise in her cheeks.

'What else did you try?' Morforwyn asked, smiling broadly, looking from one girl to the other.

'Well,' Cassie shuffled uncomfortably, 'we thought we'd try 'mermaid,' she mumbled feeling a bit embarrassed.

Morforwyn laughed and the sound was like a shower of tiny, tinkly bells which seemed to leave an echo in the air.

'I wonder what made you choose 'mermaid'.'

'Um . . . because,' Cassie took her courage in both hands and blurted out, 'You see, Morforwyn, it's because we noticed your hands were different from ours and . . . well, because of how you seem to us!' She lowered her head and toyed with the shell, feeling a bit stupid. 'We thought we'd try it, at least.' she added.

Morforwyn smiled kindly at her and raised her chin so that Cassie's eyes met hers.

'You are so sweet and almost right, my dear friends. In fact, I am half mermaid, half human. But sadly I cannot tell you everything about myself at the moment. I cannot tell you what the secret word is either, for if I speak it I risk my safety. All I can tell you is that you must look at it like a puzzle and this is what you must do.

'You need to take the first letter of each of the cottage names and you will have ten letters. These will have to be placed in the correct order to spell the name you need. The name will not be familiar to you. The only clue I can give you is that seven of the letters will spell the name of a mollusc that bores into rocks and wood. You'll need help with this. Place the three other letters in front of this word and you'll find the name to use.'

The girls nodded to each other to show they each understood. Bindy thought a while and then asked,

'Morforwyn, if we can't work out the secret word, can we ask our parents to help?'

Morforwyn looked silently out to sea for a long time, as if the sea itself was communicating with her. She turned back to the girls and said,

'Only if you really cannot do it without help, but take care not to mention me, as most grown ups do not believe in sea sprites, merfolk or other such sea creatures and you could get into trouble with them. Instead, perhaps, tell them that it's a word game you're playing and, I promise, you will be able to tell them everything when the secret is no longer a mystery. Does that satisfy you?'

Bindy nodded, she was pleased that her parents would eventually know, so she happily replied,

'Yes, thank you, Morforwyn. I suppose we'd better get back to work out the word, then?'

Morforwyn nodded but continued,

'I will add one more thing, which is very important. You will be very surprised by what you see hidden beneath the stones as they are of great value. When you collect them you must keep them hidden very safely until all are found, then you must bring them all to me and I will explain my story.'

'Do we keep our shells?' Cassie asked.

'Yes. Please keep them safe and use them as you did today to call me, and I will come to you. What you are doing is so very important to me. I earnestly thank you for all the trouble you are taking on my account. I know it can't be easy for young human children, but I believe you have the courage to succeed. I must go now.'

She turned and waved to them keeping her tail well hidden, as on the first day they met her.

CHAPTER 7

When Morforwyn had gone, Bindy and Cassie looked at each other and shared a thoughtful look. There was so much to consider.

'Come on, Cassie, let's give Trilby a walk and play with him while we work out what to do next.'

'Good idea. I suppose the first thing we have to do is to find the names of all the cottages before we can even *start* working out the name.'

They scrambled down the rocks and walked back up the beach. Trilby barked at each stick they threw for him. He was really enjoying this game! But with every throw, Bindy wondered how to get the cottage names,. She spoke her thoughts out loud,

'We can't read all the names from the path so we'll either have to go up to each door or find out if anyone knows the cottage names. Perhaps one of our parents might.'

'I don't think mine would, but we can ask.'

'*Hmm.* There is another tricky problem, of course.'

'What?'

'Well, when we've got the secret name and got this treasure stuff out from under our stones, we'll still have another eight cottage gardens to get into without being seen!'

Cassie looked worried.

'I'm not sure this is going to work out at all! I mean, we can't just go into people's gardens without a good reason.'

'Well, we'd better think of a good reason then!' laughed Bindy. After exhausting Trilby, they sat down for a while on the sand.

'What about selling something to them?' suggested Cassie.

'OK, what are you thinking of?'

'I don't know. What do people on holiday want?

'They can get most things from the mobile shop lady. Is there anything she *doesn't* sell?'

'No, she seems to sell everything, according to Mum.'

'I don't think that's going to work, then. Maybe we can offer to do something for them.'

'Like what?' Cassie asked. They both thought really hard for a bright idea but nothing came to mind.

'Well, we've got to think of something soon and I'll tell you something else.'

'What?' asked Bindy

'Most people will be going home on Saturday and they have to leave before eleven o'clock in the morning. The cleaning lady comes to get the cottages ready for the next visitors at about twelve o'clock, sometimes later.'

'How do you know that?'

'Because I overheard my Mum asking Mrs Easterson what the arrangements were for leaving here.' Cassie sighed and gazed around for inspiration.

'Oh! That's spooky.' Her attention was drawn to someone on the beach. 'Down there look, that's Mrs Easterson.'

Bindy looked down the beach to where her friend was pointing and saw a woman talking to a man who wore scruffy, working clothes. She hadn't met Mrs Easterson before and noticed that she was a slim lady with greyish, blond hair. It was tied back in a bun at her neck and she wore a long, red, tiered skirt which fluttered in the breeze. Over her skirt she wore a long, loose jumper and she carried a woven multicoloured basket. Mrs Easterson left the man with a wave goodbye and began walking up the beach. They watched her for a while but she strolled towards the dunes and the path which led back to the cottages. She looked across the beach and when she spotted Bindy and Cassie she stopped; instead of carrying on she turned and walked towards them. The girls continued to throw sticks for Trilby then, as Mrs Easterson came closer, they turned and smiled at her. Bindy noticed that her basket was completely empty and wondered to herself why she'd bothered to bring it with her.

Cassie smiled up at Mrs Easterson, shading her eyes from the sun. 'Hello', she said, 'have you been having a walk on the beach?'

'Yes, I try to walk on the beach every day. I've just been chatting to Tom, you'll probably see him a lot while you're here, helping clip the hedges and things. He also does lots of repair jobs around the village. Have you met him yet?' Mrs. Easterson had a typical Welsh voice, like a musical sound that lilted up and down as she spoke.

'No, does he live around here?' asked Cassie.

'Yes, Tom has lived in the village for a while, he's a bit of a loner though, quite shy, but very kind. He's very good at predicting the weather too—even better than the weather forecasters! He was just saying that we're going to have a good week of sunshine, which is good news, isn't it?

They nodded.

'You're Cassandra aren't you? Your mother mentioned you the other day.'

'Yes, but no-one calls me Cassandra, only if I'm being naughty! I like being called Cassie.

Mrs Easterson gathered her skirt and sat down beside them. She had quite a nice face, for someone quite old. She didn't have many lines or wrinkles, just a few around her clear blue eyes and her smile was quite pleasant.

'And are you naughty often, Cassie? Mrs Easterson enquired with a broad smile.

'Well, sometimes.' replied Cassie with a grin.

'And who is this young lady?'

'This is Bindy. She's staying in Pearl Cottage.'

'And are you both finding plenty to do here on your holidays?'

'Oh yes, it's really exciting!'

'Is it now?' replied the lady, 'and what is it that's so exciting?'

The girls looked at each other for a moment and then Bindy butted in.

'Well, we've been to a theme park and to see some caves and collected some shells and been for walks and things . . .' her voice trailed away for a moment ' . . . . actually, Mrs Easterson, you could help us, perhaps? We've just been wondering what all the cottages' names are on the hill. Do you know any of them?'

Mrs. Easterson looked at them thoughtfully.

'Well, I've lived here for a very long time and I've met all the visitors over the years so I should know, shouldn't I? Let me see . . . .' She thought a little and then said 'Now then, you're both in Pearl and Musselshell is that right?'They nodded.

'And there are ten cottages in all . . . . now there's mine, which is Kittiwake Cotta—'

'Yours?' blurted Cassie, 'I didn't realize you lived in one of these cottages, Mrs Easterson, I thought you travelled here with your mobile shop.'

'No, my dear I've lived here since I was quite a young woman and have lived in Kittiwake most of that time. I have to be by the sea, I really love it. Anyway, where were we, now? I know, let's start from the top and work down.

First is mine, Kittiwake, then there's Anemone, after the sea anemones you know, and then Lobster, Musselshell of course,' she smiled at Cassie, 'so how many is that?'

'Four' said Cassie and Bindy together.

'Right, Dolphin . . . . Pearl . . . . Oyster, that's seven . . . and then Coral and . . . . let me think . . . '

Bindy and Cassie couldn't believe their luck and glanced at each other with glee. Cassie whispered to Bindy,

'Can you remember them all?' Bindy nodded while Mrs Easterson was still thinking hard, her brow was deeply furrowed as she tried to remember the last two.

'Did I say Driftwood?'

'No.' both girls chorused. She began to recount the names on her fingers while the girls bit their lips with anticipation.

'Got it! Island, I always forget that one!' She turned and smiled at them triumphantly 'There, the old brain still works! Can you remember them all now?'

'Let's see,' said Bindy, 'Musselshell, Kittiwake and Pearl, those are easy 'cos those are ours, Oyster, Driftwood, Coral . . .' she came to a stop.

'. . . Anemone, Lobster, Dolphin,' added Cassie.

Mrs Easterson added 'and Island.'

'Island, like Great Britain.' said Bindy

'Or desert island!' added Cassie, 'Oh, Mrs Easterson, thank you so much, we can get on with . . .' Bindy dug her in the ribs.

There was an awkward silence as the girls looked at Mrs Easterson and she looked at them.

'Don't worry, girls, I shan't ask any more. I'm glad to have been of help. I must get my weary bones back up the hill now so good luck!' She got onto her knees and then got herself up, shook the sand from her skirt and picked up her basket. She turned to go with a wave and then after a couple of steps turned to look at the girls.

'If I can help again, you will ask, won't you?'

They nodded to her and watched as she walked away, back towards the dunes and the path home.

They lay back on the sand for a while watching the clouds pass idly above their heads.

'Mrs Easterson's nice, isn't she?' Bindy said, at last, turning to her friend.

'Yes, and who'd have thought we'd have all the names already! We're really lucky! Come on, it must be time to get back. Let's go and write them down so we don't forget them.' They ran towards the path calling to Trilby who bounded happily after them.

CHAPTER 8

As the girls reached Pearl Cottage, Bindy's mum greeted them with a smile. 'Oh good, I'm just about to serve supper, I'll bet you're hungry.'

'Mum, I'm absolutely starving but can I take Cassie to my room for five minutes, there's something we *must* do.'

'OK, but five minutes only.' replied Mrs Hammond firmly.

They rushed through the lounge and charged into Mr Hammond.

'Good grief, where's the fire?'

'Sorry, Dad, we're in a rush!'

'Alright, tell me all about it later.' He walked into the kitchen and sat at the table with a very perplexed expression on his face.

'I don't know about you, but I think those two are definitely up to something, they're very secretive, have you noticed? Lots of whispering and stuff.'

'Don't worry, it's probably quite innocent. It's nice that they get on so well. Didn't you have fun making new friends when you were a kid?

'I don't know, I can't remember. I don't think I did anything secretive, but maybe it's a "girl thing".' He looked at his wife enquiringly.

She smiled back at him. 'Maybe.' she said and kissed the top of his head.

Meanwhile, the girls had written all the names of the cottages in Bindy's diary. They had remembered them all and were now putting the first letters of each name in a line. When they had finished it looked extremely confusing.

M P L D O K A D I C

Bindy tore the sheet in half and wrote it out again differently for Cassie to take home. It didn't look any easier to work out that way either.

'Try to work out something from that by tomorrow and I'll do the same,' said Bindy, 'and with a bit of luck we'll be able to make some sense of it soon.' They said their goodbyes and Bindy went to join her parents at the table.

'Oh this looks delicious, Mum!'

'Good, enjoy it and there's plenty more if you want it.'

They all tucked in and after a little while Mr Hammond turned to his daughter and said, 'So what were you doing in your room that was so important?'

Bindy kept chewing for a while trying desperately to think of something to say that would not lead to too many further questions. She remembered what Morforwyn had suggested. 'Well, it's like this, Dad. Cassie and I have a puzzle to work out, all about our holiday. There are ten cottages on the hill, all with different names about the seaside. Had you realised that?' Bindy looked at her Dad with a very innocent expression and smiled at him.

'Erm, no I only know ours is Pearl or something isn't it? So what's Cassie's?'

'Musselshell. Anyway, we were writing down the names of them to see if we could make up a name from the first letters. We thought it would be fun to see if they spelt out something to do with the sea.

'Oh. I like puzzles, what are the other letters?'

'Well there's Dolphin, Island, Kittiwake, Coral and some others. I can't remember them all at the moment, that's why we had to rush back to write them down, so we wouldn't forget.' She took another mouthful and chewed slowly checking her parents' expressions. They seemed to have accepted her explanation quite well. Breathing a sigh of relief, she went on with her supper.

'What shall we do tomorrow, then?' asked Dad.

'Well, how about we visit another beach along the coast.' suggested Mum, 'Mrs Barton mentioned one the other day, didn't she? She said it had a few shops and restaurants nearby. We could make a day of it. They also do boat trips from there. If it's a nice day we could do that.'

'Do we have to go somewhere else? Why can't we stay here? Cassie and I are having so much fun.'

'We've come to visit the area, Bindy, we have to do *some* sightseeing,' explained Mum

'But we went somewhere today. Can't we do that another day?'

'Well let's see what the weather's like. If it's sunny and calm we'll go. If it's grey and breezy we'll stay around here and go for a walk along the cliffs, OK?'

'OK' agreed Bindy reluctantly.

That evening, over at Musselshell Cottage, Cassie and her parents were watching the 10 o'clock news on TV. At least Dad was. Mum was leafing through a magazine chatting away to Cassie who was busy with a piece of paper and kept ignoring her.

'What are you doing there, Cassie?'

'*Hmm?*' Cassie responded, not really listening.

'I asked what you were doing, Cassie.'

'*Erm* . . . . Puzzle.'

'Can I help?'

'*Hmm?*'

'I asked if I could help.'

'*Erm* . . . . Don't think so.'

'Where did you get it from, a book?'

'*Hmm?*'

'Oh, for goodness' sake, Cassie, put it down for a moment and talk to me properly.'

Cassie looked up and gave her mother her full attention.

'Sorry. It's just a word puzzle, Mum. I thought I'd try to work it out before bed.'

Well, I'd like to help if you get stuck. Is it a crossword puzzle?'

'No. I've got to make a name out of ten letters and it's tricky. I need to concentrate.'

'Alright, I'll leave you to it but if you want help, just ask.'

'OK. Thanks.'

Cassie was finding it really, really, tricky.

All she'd got so far was DIM PADLOCK, PAMLIDDOCK or DICK OD PALM then she realised Dick was a man's name so it couldn't be Dick—something for a mollusc. Whoever heard of a mollusc called Dick!

Then she started working out what the other letters might spell. Did any of this sound like the name of a mollusc? She wasn't really sure. She yawned loudly.

'Good heavens, you sound like the gorilla from Bristol Zoo!' said her father.

'Oh thanks, Dad,' she responded, 'at least I don't *look* like him!'

'Are you suggesting that *I*, the most handsome of men, look like a gorilla?'

'Well, now that you mention it . . .' she laughed.

'Cheeky blooming monkey!'

'Cheeky gorilla!' she retorted and went over to give him a hug. 'I'm tired. I'm going to bed. Goodnight, Dad.'

'Goodnight, Princess.' he said.

'Did you work out the puzzle, love?' asked her mother as Cassie bent to kiss her goodnight.

No, but I'm not giving up yet.' She gave her mum a cheerful smile, picked up the piece of paper and went into her bedroom.

CHAPTER 9

Cassie and Bindy were stirring up a big pot they'd found on the beach over a blazing fire and inside it were lots of letters of the alphabet. Bindy was mixing them around to make special words but they kept flying out of the pot into the air. Even though Cassie tried to run after them she couldn't catch them, they were just out of reach. Mrs Easterson had been trying to catch them in her basket but they kept flying away from her, too.

'It's nine o'clock,' said Mrs Easterson, 'we have to leave soon.'

'But we can't leave the letters on the beach, they'll be lost forever!'

'It's nine o'clock, Cassie!'

'I *can't* leave!'

'Cassie, Cassie wake up, it's nine o'clock!' said her mother.

Cassie blinked and sighed gratefully. It had been a dream, a mad, frantic dream.

'The puzzle!' she thought, *'it must have been about the puzzle.'*

'Are you alright, love?' asked Mum

Cassie yawned.

'Yeah, Mum, I was just having a crazy dream. Bindy and I were on the beach and Mrs Easterson was in it. She was telling us it was nine o'clock and we had to leave.'

'That was me, actually. It *is* nine o'clock and we *do* have to leave.'

'Why, where are we going?'

'Well, as it's pouring with rain, as you can hear, we thought rather than stay here we'd go into town and spend the day there. What do you think?'

'It's a bit boring.'

'Not at all,' said her mother 'there are lots of places to see and things to do. If the rain keeps on we can go to the cinema, there's a Playzone, a Leisure Centre and shops to buy presents—you could spend some of your holiday money. Is that OK?' She waited for a positive response from Cassie and when none came she added, 'We may as well, love, not much to do in here or on the beach in this weather.'

'Can Bindy come?'

'I don't know, Cass, they may have plans of their own and I'm not sure Bindy's parents would want her to come with us all day, we don't know each other *that* well yet and they probably want to have a day on their own.'

Cassie looked disappointed.

'Can I just go over and see her before I go, then? I'd like to arrange to meet her later.'

'Yes of course, but get up and have breakfast first,'

Cassie got washed and dressed and went to eat her breakfast. She had her secret puzzle in her pocket to show Bindy.

Back in Pearl Cottage, Bindy and her parents had decided that as it was such a wet day they'd abandon the plans they'd made yesterday as they couldn't do a boat trip or walk on the cliffs. Bindy was sitting, staring out at the raindrops on the window when she heard a knock at the door. Mum went over to open it.

'Hello Cassie, come in out of the rain. Isn't it horrible weather? Are you going anywhere today?'

'Yes, that's why I came over. We're going to town today. It's got a Leisure Centre, Play Zone, shops and things so as I'll be away most of the day so I wondered if Bindy and I could meet up later.'

'That sounds like a good day out. We could do that, Frank?' she said looking at her husband.

Dad was in his newspaper again. *'Hmm?'* Dad was always absorbed by the news.

Mum looked exasperated 'Bindy, would *you* like to do that?'

The girls looked at each other with delight.

'Would I? Course I would! We could take our swimming costumes and have a swim and then play in the Play Zone. Great!'

'And what about the Dads and Mums?' piped up Dad. He *had* been listening after all.

'Well, we can all swim and we can sit with the Bartons and chat while the girls play in the 'Zone.'

'Alright, but I don't think we should impose on the Bartons all day. We need to do a few things too.'

'Yes, that's fine, I certainly need to shop for a few things and we can do something you'd like to do, too. How does that sound?'

'Fine.' said Dad. 'What time shall we meet at the swimming pool, eleven o'clock? It will take us a while to get ourselves organised.'

'Look,' said Mum, 'I'll go and speak to the Bartons and make arrangements while you two get your costumes and towels together . . . AND DON'T FORGET MINE!' she called, as she walked out through the door with Cassie.

Half an hour later the Hammonds had organised themselves and were in the car. Both parents had been pleased to meet up for the girls to play together and Cassie had been allowed to travel in Bindy's car. This gave them the opportunity to compare puzzle notes.

They showed each other what they'd worked out and both had come up with similar words which didn't make much sense to either of them. From her bag Bindy took out a little book called 'The British Seashore.' which was all about the different types of seashore plants and sea life. It had illustrations as well as names in English, and a strange language, which her dad explained was Latin.

'Where did you get that?' asked Cassie.

'It was on a shelf in my bedroom with a lot of other books, I brought it with me to see if we could recognise any names.'

'Perfect!'

They pored over the index. *Encrusting lichens, Green seaweeds, Introduction to worms',* they made a face at each other in disgust, *'Introduction to molluscs . . . . page 86.'* They pointed excitedly to the section at the same time. Bindy turned to the page and they began to read together quietly *'There is a huge variety of molluscs . . . . some of which live in freshwater but most are marine. The several classes all look very different but all have a muscular foot called a mantle . . . '*

'This is going to take forever!'

'How many pages are there on molluscs?' Cassie asked. Bindy checked quickly.

'Twenty.' she sighed and made a face.

Cassie wriggled onto her side and brought out her paper again.

'Let's look for names like the ones we've worked out.'

'Good idea.'

Luckily, all the names were written in bold print so were easily readable. They checked the ones they'd worked out but found nothing at all to resemble them. There were a couple of names which contained some of the letters but also included letters which they didn't have. There were so many of them Bindy began to feel car sick. She put the book down and asked her Dad to play her favourite music CD. After a little while Cassie picked the book up and carried on checking from where they'd left off. She discovered so many names for molluscs; *small periwinkle, rough periwinkle, flat periwinkle*, and those were just periwinkles! *Common wendletrap, banded chink, cowries,* this was a mystery in itself. Then all of a sudden Cassie gave a little gasp and read out in a whisper,

' . . . *the brittle delicate shell of the Common Piddock is surprisingly strong, boring into slate, chalk, wood and hard clays* . . . .

She got out her pencil and ticked off the letters one by one; P . . . yes, I . . . yes . . . Two Ds . . . yes . . . O . . . C . . . K . . . . yes, yes and YES! *Seven letters we've got it!*

She nudged Bindy who looked at the paper and gave the thumbs up sign. The other letters left un-ticked were LM and A so by shuffling these letters around they were left with a choice of, ALM, AML, MLA, MAL, LMA, or LAM Piddock. They both felt happy and excited. They were going to solve this, they just knew it.

Chapter 10

Both families enjoyed an extremely enjoyable day despite the rain. They spent an hour in the swimming pool which had a great water slide and wave machine. After that, they went on to the Play Zone and the girls exhausted themselves on huge slides and massive climbing frames, by which time they were all ready to head for lunch at one of the town's seaside restaurants.

Having spent quite a few hours together, Bindy and Cassie had managed to do a bit of planning ahead for the next stage in their treasure hunt. They decided that they'd get together that night and try to open one stone only. They remembered everything that Morforwyn had told them even down to choosing a bag in which to put the treasure.

Each cottage had a supply of plastic chairs, loungers and an umbrella housed in its own garden shed which also held other gardening bits and pieces. While getting the chairs out one day, Bindy had noticed an old fashioned shopping bag, full of cobwebs, dust and spiders, scrunched up in a dark corner of their shed. This is what they were going to use. If there was anywhere someone would *not* look for treasure, it was in that ghastly bag! They decided to toss a coin for who was to shake the spiders out and it fell to Bindy to complete this task. She didn't mind, she wasn't scared of creepy crawlies like Cassie and anyway, this was an adventure, wasn't it?

After lunch at the restaurant the families had gone their separate ways. By 6 o'clock, Cassie and her parents were making their way back to the cottage. As soon as they arrived, Cassie scribbled a short note and ran across to Pearl Cottage, posting it through Bindy's bedroom window, which was slightly ajar. It just said '*See you by your stone at 1a.m, I'll bring a torch.*'

When Bindy eventually got home she was feeling quite excited already but when she got to her room and read the note she felt her heart jump into her throat. All sorts of feelings were running through her head and she felt so jittery she had to go outside and breathe some fresh air to make her feel calmer. They'd both agreed to try three versions of the name; Lampiddock, Almpiddock and Malpiddock as the other variations didn't seem to sound right. They didn't actually think *any* of them made sense but this was their plan.

The evening seemed to last an eternity for the girls. Each, in their own way, tried to take their minds off their adventure, by reading, watching TV or playing music. Eventually it was time for them to go to bed. They both lay in their beds, fully clothed apart from their shoes, thinking of how the other must be feeling and desperately hoping this plan would go well. Time dragged by. On one occasion, Bindy felt herself drifting off to sleep but she jerked herself awake and sat up to look at the clock. 12.30—half an hour to go!

Cassie, meanwhile, was sitting up reading a comic with her Dad's torch which she'd taken from the car earlier when her parents weren't looking. She was getting so tense and edgy that she decided she couldn't wait any longer. She'd heard her father snoring a while ago and hoped her mum was fast asleep too.

She slipped on her trainers and a warm fleece and opened the window of her bedroom very gently. She took two spare pillows from the wardrobe and stuffed them into her bed to make it look as if she was in there, fast asleep. Then she picked up the torch and made sure it was off as she didn't want to attract attention yet. She looked around outside the window to see if there was anyone watching or passing along the path. There was no-one there so she started to climb out very quietly and slowly, watching and listening with every movement. Suddenly, she heard something. She stopped dead and held her breath. It was a creaking sound coming from her garden. She leant forward and strained her eyes to see what it was. It was the gate, not quite on its latch. She must have rushed so much after getting the torch that she'd forgotten to close it properly! She slowly let out a big breath. Her heart was beating so loudly, she felt her parents or the cats must be able to hear the *thump, thump, thump* banging in her ears. *'Calm down,'* she told herself sternly, *'or you'll ruin it all.'* She was on the window ledge outside her room and all she had left to do was to jump down about a metre onto the grass. *'Down at last!'* She crouched there for a moment to listen then slowly made for the gate. She was through! This time she closed the gate properly.

Creeping low past the other cottages she soon got to Bindy's gate and undid the latch. It was a bit stiff and made a dull clunking sound. She hid behind it for a moment to see if a light would go on but it was alright, she was lucky. Keeping her head down she moved stealthily into the garden towards Bindy's window then raised herself a little, peeped in and saw the shadow of Bindy in bed. She gave a little tap and whispered,

'It's only me. Come on, its all clear.'

Bindy rushed to the window, and whispered back,

'I thought we said 1 o'clock!'

'We did, I just couldn't wait any longer.' She gave Bindy a helpless look. 'Come on, I'll help you down.'

In no time at all Bindy was stuffing her own bed with pillows and had put her shoes and a jumper on. She grabbed the old shopping bag which she'd managed to secrete in her room after cleaning it. Once on the ground, she and Cassie crept slowly and nervously around to the front of the cottage. The stars were out and sparkling brightly and a crescent moon hung in the sky. A wild animal screeched, probably a fox, and they felt a shiver run down their spines.

They turned and crept towards the cottage door. Bindy reached up, took hold of the pearl and pulled gently but firmly until the bone key was released. The pearl was in her hand. Motioning to each other to keep silent, they slowly and steadily reached the special stone. Bindy's hand was shaking as she placed the 'key' into the opening. Cassie could see she was nervous and placed her own hand on top to steady her. Together they moved the key into the slot, guiding it into position. Again, it stopped half way and so Bindy guided it left and right until, *click*, the key found its home and the pearl sank into place neatly. The girls looked at each other and silently mouthed the first name they'd chosen to try. After giving each other an encouraging nod, they announced in a loud whisper,

'LAMPIDDOCK.'

They waited. Nothing happened. They looked at each other and mouthed their second choice. With another nod they whispered the name,

'ALMPIDDOCK.'

Again, nothing. This time they crossed their fingers and looking at each other intently spoke the third name together in a clear, loud, whisper.

'MALPIDDOCK.'

Suddenly, the stone sprang open with a strong, mysterious, force and, as it did so, the girls were flung backwards and let out gasps of shock. With the unexpectedness of their fall, they had let go of the pearl and were sprawled together in a heap. They sat up quickly and saw that the pearl key was glowing with many colours, casting a rainbow of light around them. They stared at each other in awe and gazing at Cassie, Bindy whispered, *'Magic!'*

Despite feeling scared, the girls crawled over to the hole and, turning on the torch, peered inside to see what was there. The hole was only about thirty centimetres deep and lying at the bottom was a small pouch, made of some strange material. Cassie reached in with trembling fingers and brought it out. The pouch felt like soft scaly leather and it was quite heavy. She opened it wide enough for Bindy to see and held it towards the light of the torch.

Inside were lots of large round pearls in gorgeous colours; black, grey, pink, green, blue, cream. They were undoubtedly the biggest and most beautiful pearls in the world, shimmering as brightly as the stars. The girls shared a look of wonder and amazement and gazed back at the treasure they'd uncovered. All of a sudden, the radiance from the pearl key faded and they were plunged once again into darkness. Bindy shivered. Cassie quickly replaced the pearls in their pouch and opening the old shopping bag, gently lowered the treasure inside. Safely zipped up, they placed it on the ground near them while they both moved the stone back down into place. There had been a breeze building up and the girls worked quickly when, out of the silence, there was an almighty *BANG!*

'What was that?' Bindy cried, absolutely terrified, and looked across to where the noise had come from.

'*BANG!*' it went again, louder this time. Inside the cottage Trilby started barking.

'Oh no!' said Cassie realising her mistake, 'I left your gate open and the wind is banging it against the post.'

While Cassie was picking up her torch a light went on inside the cottage. She switched it off quickly. Bindy hastily took hold of the pearl key and removed it gently from the stone.

'Quick, in here,' she said and ran towards the door of the shed.

Safe inside, they held the door shut with the tips of their fingers and crouched down. Their heads were just below the small window so Bindy gradually peeped out to see what was happening. She saw her father coming out of the cottage in his pyjamas, holding a torch with Trilby at his heels. He walked onto the grass, flashing the torch around the garden and sweeping its light across the front of the shed. They ducked lower and waited. From a corner of the window, Bindy risked another look. Disaster! He was walking across the garden towards the shed. Just as he was reaching the door, the gate banged again. He turned towards the sound, walked back towards the side of the house and shut the gate. Checking it was secure, he called Trilby and went back indoors.

'*Phew*, that was close!' whispered Bindy.

Cassie nodded.

They stayed in the shed and waited a few moments for the light to go off again. When it did, they checked they'd picked up everything and walked quickly to the name plate. Bindy eased the pearl key back into place, turned to Cassie, who was beside her carrying the bag, and motioned to her to follow her. They ran, crouching under the windows, until they got to Bindy's bedroom.

She took a peep into her room. *Oh no!* Her door was opening! Her father was poking his head around the door and was looking inside to check on her! She waited, pushing Cassie's head down as her friend was trying to get up. Bindy was praying the pillows would disguise her body sufficiently. Holding her breath, she waited for what seemed an age before, at last, the door closed again. She released her hand from Cassie's head.

'What's going on?' Cassie whispered.

'My dad just checked my room!' Bindy whispered back.

'Really? Has he gone?'

'Yes, thank goodness!'

'Good. What shall we do with the bag, though?' whispered Cassie. The plan had been to leave it in the shed but, with all the unforeseen confusion, Cassie still held it tightly to her chest.

'What if I hide it in my bedroom tonight,' suggested Bindy, 'then we can decide what to do tomorrow?'

Cassie nodded. She waited for Bindy to open her window and climb back inside then passed the bag up to her.

'Don't forget the gate, Cassie!' Bindy warned quietly. Cassie gazed back, crossing her heart and made her way back to Musselshell Cottage, this time making absolutely sure she closed each gate carefully behind her.

Relieved to be back, she ran to her bedroom window to find everything was quiet and normal. As she climbed back inside she looked out at her garden and wondered what treasures they'd uncover tomorrow.

CHAPTER 11

'Bindy.' Mum called gently, drawing back the curtains. 'Time to rise and shine.' Bindy yawned and stretched.

'What time's it?' she asked sleepily and then immediately remembered last night and that she had a bag of pearls stashed under her bed. Mum looked at her watch.

'It's just gone half past nine. You're very sleepy this morning, did you sleep alright?'

'Yes, but I didn't get to sleep straight away.'

'Dad had to get up in the night, did you hear him?'

'No. Why, what was the matter?'

'Oh just the gate outside banging in the wind, I'm surprised you didn't hear it—it certainly woke us up. Dad came and checked on you but he said you were fast asleep and buried under the covers.'

Bindy felt rather relieved that their plan had worked. She looked out of the window. The wind from last night seemed to have died down as she watched the leaves on the trees moving gently. The day was bright and sunny and despite wanting to get up she still felt rather tired so she sank back under the duvet where it was cosy and warm.

'Oh, no sign of you moving, then,' smiled her Mum on her way out, 'I'll leave you to get up in your own time. Dad and I are taking it easy this morning and sitting outside in the sunshine. Breakfast is on the table when you want it.'

'Thanks Mum.'

Bindy lay her head on the pillows thinking about last night and all the amazing things that had happened. She reached under the bed and felt for the bag. Yes, it was still there. She pulled it out and looked inside, fixing her gaze on the pouch. She couldn't resist another look so pulled it out and opened it under the duvet letting in a chink of light. Yes, they were still there in all their glory. She put her fingers into the bag and felt their smooth coldness touching her warm hand. She brought one out and held it up to the light. It was creamy white, heavy and a perfect sphere. She remembered her grandmother telling her once, when she was showing Bindy some of her jewellery, that you could identify a real pearl by rubbing it against your teeth. If it made your tooth feel rough, it was a real pearl. Bindy didn't doubt this pearl was real but tested it anyway. She felt a definite roughness and touched her tooth with her tongue to reassure herself that her tooth wasn't damaged!

She put it back with the others and then back under the bed inside the shopping bag. She thought for a while about where they were going to hide it. Her parents often went into the shed so maybe that wasn't such a good idea. She looked around her room. Wardrobe, drawer, suitcase . . . yes, her suitcase was a possibility. It had a number lock on it which would only open if someone knew the number. If the treasure was put in there it would be safe. She closed her eyes again and decided that this might be as good a place as any for now.

Meanwhile, back at Musselshell Cottage, Cassie sat up in bed and felt really satisfied about last night. She considered herself extremely brave, too. Not many kids her age would even think of doing what they did last night, not even boys. She felt rather proud of herself, except for the gate, of course, that was a complete disaster! What next? A visit to Bindy's! She got up, washed and dressed and went to see if her parents were awake. They were in the kitchen having breakfast.

'We didn't call you,' said Mum, 'because you were sleeping so deeply we thought you'd appreciate a lie-in.'

'What time is it?' Cassie asked.

'Nearly ten o'clock, you must be hungry. I'll make you some scrambled eggs.'

Cassie realised that she was absolutely famished so helped by putting toast in the toaster. After a minute or two it popped and she spread two pieces of toast with butter and took a big bite.

'Mmm . . . delicious,' she sighed pleasurably, 'I could eat a horse.'

'Stay back, cats, dangerous, animal-eating child on the loose!' said Dad, in his favourite Batman voice. Simba was rubbing his head against Cassie's leg and Sandy was staring up at the table, wiggling her back ready to launch herself onto it. Cassie pushed her away gently with the back of her hand and gave Simba a rub with her foot.

'What are we doing today?' she asked.

'You can do anything you want to do,' said Dad, 'but I'm playing golf.'

'I thought if we weren't going anywhere I'd get Bindy to come over and have a girly day together.'

'Oh yes,' said Dad, 'and what will that mean?'

'I'm not sure yet, maybe do each other's hair, paint our nails, read some comics, you know, that sort of thing.'

'Well, I'm definitely not going to be here if you're painting nails. That stuff stinks!'

'Here you are, eat up.' said Mum, placing a steaming plate of scrambled eggs in front of her. 'I have to buy a few things food-wise, do you want anything?'

'Um, no, don't think so.' Cassie replied. 'Is it warm out?'

'It's not too bad. We could go down the beach later and have a long walk to the next cove before the tide comes back in. I need to stretch my legs a bit.'

'If you stretch them any more, they'll twang!' Dad chortled.

Her mother tutted and rolled her eyes. Cassie smiled up at her mum.

'I'd like a walk later, too, but can Bindy come over just for an hour or two this morning?'

'Yes, OK. If you like you can both come with me to the shop, while Dad goes off to play golf.'

'Great, I'll go over and tell her.' She drank down some juice and skipped happily down the lane.

On arriving at Bindy's, Cassie discovered that Mr Hammond was going to play golf with her Dad, so that left just the Mums to keep occupied while they opened the stone at their cottage. Mrs Hammond said she had some postcards to send so she, also, needed to go up to see Mrs Easterson. They decided they'd all go together.

An hour later, they were sitting on a wooden bench in the car park at the top of the hill waiting for the mobile shop to arrive. Luckily, it was a nice day and they were enjoying the warmth of the sun when, '*toot toot*', the mobile shop trundled along the stony road and came to a stop at its usual parking place. Mrs Easterson got out of the drivers cab and walked to the back to open up the doors for custom.

'Good morning, ladies. Lovely morning.'

'Yes, isn't it warm? It would be great if this lasted a few more days.' replied Mrs Hammond.

'Well, the forecast is good, so let's hope so.' smiled Mrs Easterson, letting the mums into the shop. The girls followed as Mrs Easterson moved further in behind the small counter area which backed onto the driver's cab. They looked around the shop which was crammed full of all sorts of weird and wonderful things. There were items of food for cats and dogs as well as for people. Drinks of all sorts in cans and bottles, fruit and vegetables stacked high, a freezer with fish, meat and more vegetables and hanging from the ceiling from hooks were buckets, nets, spades, inflatable boats and rings, bats and balls and beach games then, near the counter, was a range of postcards, newspapers and magazines, comics, sweets and chocolate. It was a real Aladdin's cave. The girls couldn't believe it. From the outside it didn't look as if it would hold so much. Mrs. Easterson was watching them.

'So what are you girls going to do today?'

'We're going to play in Cassie's garden,' replied Bindy, absorbed by the games which hung from the roof.

'Mum, can we buy one of these ball games, please?' She was pointing to a box showing a ball on elastic attached to a tall stand and it included two bats which meant the girls could play together. Mrs Hammond looked at it for a moment.

'Swing ball! I used to play that game, its great fun. How much is it Mrs Easterson?'

'Let's see,' she grabbed a long stick with a grabber at the end and released the game from its hook.

'Now then,' she turned the set over and showed them the ticket price.

'We'll take it,' smiled Mrs. Hammond, 'I might have a go myself!'

Mrs. Easterson took it over to the counter and rang it up on the till, then reached down to find a bag for it. As she did so, the girls were able to look into the driver's cab. Cassie bent towards Bindy and gave her a sharp nudge and nodded towards the dashboard. Bindy followed Cassie's eyes and saw what she'd noticed. Standing against the front windscreen was a photograph of a young girl with very long hair and it looked remarkably like Morforwyn.

Mrs Easterson straightened up from her search and the girls noticed she was watching them. She put the game in the bag and waited for the mums to finish their shopping. Mrs. Easterson rang up the totals on her till and they paid her. All the while Mrs Easterson watched the girls with a very strange look in her eyes.

CHAPTER 12

As they walked back down the hill, Bindy and Cassie began speculating about the photograph. What on earth was going on? Did Morforwyn know Mrs Easterson? They didn't know what to believe. It was making everything even more complicated. If Morforwyn wanted help and Mrs Easterson *was* her friend why hadn't she done all this treasure hunting; she had every opportunity. They were very confused indeed.

Eventually they got their shopping back to the cottages and the girls got busy setting up the game in Cassie's garden. It didn't take long and they placed it near the stone so that they could take their chance in opening it quickly to reach the treasure.

They enjoyed playing for about an hour and were really getting the hang of it. Mrs Hammond came up the path as she'd been invited over to spend the afternoon with Mrs Barton while their husbands were golfing. Trilby was with her so she asked Bindy to keep him in the garden with them while she went inside. This was rather fortunate as the door would be kept firmly shut in case the cats got out or Trilby got in!

They went to get themselves a drink and sat down on the grass to cool down after their game. Everything inside the cottage was quiet so they decided to try and open the stone straight away. They checked what their mums were doing and found that they were chatting and having a cup of tea in the lounge, which looked out over the sea, while the girls were at the side of the house and not easily visible from the path or the window. Just in case, Cassie opened the garden umbrella out in front of the stone and dug the spokes into the soft grass so that it wouldn't blow over. She'd also grabbed a carrier bag from the kitchen to put the treasure in, so they were all set. They finished their drinks and put them back in the kitchen.

On her way out, Cassie removed the mussel shell key. Once released and in her hand, she walked quickly over to the stone and crouched next to Bindy behind the umbrella. Trilby, always interested in something new, sat down next to them. She placed the 'key' into the hole and pushed down. Again there was resistance but after changing direction she felt it slot into place. They held it together and whispered,

'*MALPIDDOCK!*'

The stone suddenly shot open, but the girls were prepared for it this time having positioned themselves either side of it and for that reason kept their balance. The stone shell glowed an intense blue. Trilby had jumped back and now tilted his head from side to side quizzically and gave a low growl. He gradually came nearer sniffing around the hole. They all leaned over the edge and peered inside. There lay yet another pouch made from the same type of leathery material as before. Cassie reached in, lifted it out and her fingers closed around a solid heavy shape.

'It's heavy,' she whispered, 'we need to get this inside so that we can look at it properly without anyone seeing.'

Bindy agreed, so she held the carrier bag open and Cassie placed the treasure inside. They moved the stone back gently and then Cassie, very carefully, removed the stone key.

'What about Trilby,' asked Bindy, 'we can't take him in with us?'

Cassie looked around and noticed a long piece of rope which she'd been using as a skipping rope.

'Here, put him on his lead and attach this rope to it. We can tie it onto that tree and he can run around the garden safely.'

'Good idea.'

They quickly replaced the umbrella, put the mussel shell key back in place and everything was back to normal. As they walked into the kitchen, Cassie shouted to her Mum,

'We're just going into my room for a bit, OK, Mum?'

'OK,' called Mrs Barton and resumed her conversation with Mrs Hammond.

The girls sat on the bed and opened up the carrier bag. Bindy lifted out the pouch and found it was really heavy, like Cassie had said. When she opened it they both gasped as the blue glow continued to shimmer from inside the bag. She took a gulp, reached in and felt inside. She touched the object and thought it would feel warm because of the glow but it was cold and smooth with some ridges over it. She lifted it out and placed it in Cassie's hands.

It was the shiniest metal she had ever seen. It was very highly polished and heavy like gold but the colour was a deep, rich blue. She was holding a beautiful mussel shell and it was engraved with patterns and encrusted with tiny jewels which followed the flowing contours of the shell. As it caught the light from the window it sparkled so much the girls were mesmerized by its beauty.

'Isn't it fabulous?' whispered Bindy, eventually.

Cassie looked up. 'I can't believe this is happening. I'm getting a bit worried. This must be worth a fortune.'

'Do you think we ought to tell our parents?' asked Bindy.

'Yes. No . . . Not yet, OK? Let's see if the others are as valuable first. If they are, maybe we ought to see Morforwyn.

'Yes, I think you're right.'

'Where will you hide it, Cassie?'

'In my rucksack. I'll wrap it all in some tissue first. It's somewhere my parents never look so it will be safe, I promise.'

'Good, then once we've got more we'll need to keep them together. We also need to start looking in the other cottage gardens. That's the really tricky bit. What day is it today?'

'Er, Wednesday.'

'That means most people will be going home on Saturday morning which is in three days' time. We'll have to work quickly! Maybe, if we're lucky, some people will go home on Friday afternoon. That may give us extra time before any new people arrive.'

'But how are we going to find out who's staying and who's going?'

'We need a good reason to visit them and find out when they're leaving. We need to think of something everyone will want us to do for them.'

They thought hard for some minutes.

'What if we offer to wash their cars for them?' Cassie said. 'Ours was really dusty and dirty when we arrived and Dad thought of taking it to a car wash before going home. I wonder if they'll let us do that.'

'We'd have to be really cheap so that they say yes. How much are car washes?'

'Dad pays £5, I think.'

'What about £1 a car, they're bound to say yes to that?'

'Do you think so?'

'Well, we'd be much cheaper than a car wash! Even *I* could afford that price! We'll ask them when they're going so that we can wash their cars the day before they leave. We can tell them we're doing it to buy presents for our parents; they're bound to agree to that!'

'OK. Let's start tomorrow morning.'

'Deal.' smiled Bindy and they gave each other a high-five.

'Right, first of all we need to get some stuff to wash cars with. What would we need?'

'Well,' said Bindy, 'my dad usually uses a bucket and puts some washing-up liquid in it.'

'What does he use for a cloth?'

'I don't know. Let's go and ask.'

Cassie put the treasure bag in her rucksack while Bindy went into the lounge where the mums were still talking.

'Mum, what things would we need to wash cars?'

Her mother paused in mid-chat looking at her with surprise and asked the obvious question.

'What do you want to know for?'

'We thought we'd ask all the people in the cottages whether they'd like us to clean their cars before going back home. We wanted to earn some extra pocket money without asking you for it all the time.' Cassie came in and sat on the sofa.

Mrs Barton turned to Mrs Hammond and smiled, 'Well that's rather enterprising of them, don't you think?' They laughed together in the way grown—ups do when they think they know more about things than their children.

'Well,' prompted Cassie, 'what do we need, then?'

'You need a large bucket and sponge each, lots of water to clean the surface dirt off, plenty of soapy water to wash off the stubborn dirt, lots of rinsing water and a cloth to wipe dry and polish. If you're going to wax them you need extra cloths and wax, of course.'

'Gosh, have we got any of that stuff?'

'We've got buckets, soap, water and cloths' added Mrs Hammond 'but no sponges; you'll need large ones otherwise it'll take for ever.'

The girls thought about where they might find these elusive sponges.

'I wonder if Mrs Easterson has any.' Bindy suggested.

'Yes, come on, let's go back up and see if she's still there . . . er, money, Mum?' smiled Cassie

'Always a catch!' responded Mrs Barton, 'I expect to be paid back out of the profits, mind.' She smiled at her daughter and winked.

In five minutes they were back up at the top of the hill and Mrs Easterson's big van was still parked in its spot. They climbed in and found her serving a couple of children with sweets. The girls looked around for what they wanted but couldn't find sponges anywhere.

'Hello again girls, what can I do for you?'

'We need large sponges please. We want to raise some pocket money by washing cars for all the holiday makers.'

Mrs Easterson looked around and thought hard.

'Now then, let's see. I've got some somewhere.' She pottered around for a while.

'Aha! I knew I had some,' and she brought out, from the depths of a corner, a box of large, colourful sponges. 'How many did you want?'

'One each, please.'

'Right, choose your colours.' She waited while Cassie chose a yellow one and Bindy a pink one.

'That's £1.50 please, girls. You're going to be busy then, washing cars for people.'

They smiled, handed over the money and turned to go.

'Wait girls, there's something in the cab I want to show you.' She wriggled into the driver's seat and looked inside her glove compartment.

'Have you seen one of these before?' She opened her hand and there shining brightly sat a little green shell exactly the same as the ones Morforwyn had given them.

CHAPTER 13

The girls didn't say anything. They were too dumbstruck to even look at each other. Mrs Easterson's voice remained low but clear.

'It's alright, my dears, you know you can trust me, don't you?' She held their gaze and looked quite serious. Cassie looked up at Mrs Easterson. She wasn't sure about the way she was looking at them. She cleared her throat and said,

'What do you mean, Mrs Easterson, trust you about what?'

'I think you know. I think you've seen shells like this before, haven't you?'

'It's very pretty, but no, we haven't, how much is it?' Cassie asked looking perfectly innocent.

Mrs Easterson laughed. Bindy began feeling nervous.

'Sorry, Mrs Easterson,' she said, 'we've got to go. Lots to do, you know. Thanks for showing us the shell.'

She dragged Cassie by the arm and practically pulled her through the door. Once out of the van they ran down the path, nearly bumping into Tom, who was pushing a heavy wheelbarrow back up the hill. They mumbled a quick apology, turned and looked back briefly at Mrs Easterson who stood at the top of the hill watching them. She was waving and shouting something but they couldn't quite hear her. Bindy felt a shiver run through her despite the warm sun on their backs.

They ran until they reached Musselshell Cottage and sat on the grass breathing heavily, waiting to see if Mrs Easterson would follow them. She didn't, but the situation was getting tricky. Would she tell their parents about it? How much did she know? Was she a friend of Morforwyn's or not? All these questions and more came bubbling out of the girls but, of course, they had no answers. They carried on discussing their situation for a while and they began to feel calmer.

'What do we do, Bindy?' Cassie asked.

'I don't know, Cassie. Maybe it's time we told our parents.'

'Do you really think so?'

'Well, if Mrs Easterson is a friend of Morforwyn she'll want to help, won't she? If she's not and wants to get to Morforwyn through us, she may be dangerous and blow all the hard work we've done already. Morforwyn told us not to tell *anyone* . . . . oh Cassie, I don't know! I wish we'd never started this; it's too much for us. We're not grown ups and I'm beginning to wish I'd never heard of Morforwyn!'

'Don't say that, Bindy. There's got to be an answer. Perhaps we should go and see Morforwyn. She'll tell us if she's a friend or not.'

'That's true', Bindy thought, Cassie was right, there *was* always Morforwyn. She began to feel a bit happier. 'Yes, come on, let's go and see her now!'

They explained to their mothers that they were going to the beach and, as usual, had to take Trilby along too. They grabbed some crisps and wandered down the lane in a very uncertain frame of mind.

As soon as they got onto the beach they saw a figure, quite far away but they knew it was Mrs Easterson because she was wearing her red billowy skirt and she had her basket on her arm again. They had both realised this at the same time and grabbed each other, flattening themselves behind a large rock to stay out of sight. Their hearts were beating wildly. Cassie pulled Bindy forward a little to spy on her so that they could see where she was but they'd been mistaken, she was actually further away so must have been walking towards the *sea* not towards *them*. They felt a slight sense of relief but decided to look for a better place to hide in order to stay safe and keep an eye on her at the same time.

The trouble was that Trilby was desperate to run around and was pulling away from Bindy, who held him firmly by the collar. Keeping him tied to one spot was not going to be easy. They kept peeping to see what Mrs Easterson was doing and found to their horror that she was climbing near the very rocks where Morforwyn was! They moved forward very slowly and decided to run towards the sand dunes where they could hide but also have a good view of what was happening. Putting Trilby on his lead and enticing him with some crisps, they waited for Mrs Easterson to move out of sight and then they ran along the beach and up behind the sand dunes. Crouching as low as they could, they found a perfect sandy spot hidden by tall, coarse grass. They lay down on their tummies and waited.

They were there for about half an hour but there was no sign of the woman. Trilby was beginning to whine and they were running out of crisps to keep him quiet.

'This is hopeless!' Cassie complained, 'what can she be doing?'

'She must know Morforwyn, but as a friend or what?'

'I don't know but we can't stay here for much longer, Trilby's been so good but we may have to come down another day. Poor dog, he must be fed up.'

Bindy gave him a loving pat and stroked his silky head.

'Quick, get down!' Cassie whispered, grabbing Bindy's arm.

Mrs Easterson was coming down from the rocks. Half way down she stopped and stood up looking around her. There were a few other people on the beach walking and playing games. The girls kept their heads low then after a few moments looked up again to see where she was. She'd disappeared *again*.

'Where's she gone *now*?' they whispered, panic rising in their voices.

'I can't see her anywhere.' said Bindy.

'Nor me, she couldn't have moved *that* fast! It's impossible! Unless she scrambled back up to the cave but she would have to have been very quick!' The girls lay still but continued to watch for signs of her.

After some time had passed, they decided to go home. This had not been the successful quest for information they'd been hoping for but there was now no doubt that this person was aware of the cave and probably Morforwyn. She knew, or at least, had some suspicion that they had met the mermaid and maybe she was trying to find out how much they knew. They agreed that they would have to avoid Mrs Easterson from now on until they learned the truth from Morforwyn but today was not the day. It was too dangerous. They decided to return when this woman was busy elsewhere.

Very slowly they raised themselves onto their knees and stood up, still watching the beach carefully. There had been no sign of Mrs Easterson anywhere which added to the mystery surrounding her. They turned away from the beach to clamber down from the dunes and head for home and as they did so they gasped in shock—there on the sand in front of them was Mrs Easterson's basket! It was unmistakeably hers; the girls had seen it so many times. They stared at it for some time and noticed that inside was a piece of folded paper held down by a shell, the green shiny shell.

CHAPTER 14

Bindy and Cassie knelt down beside the basket looking around for Mrs Easterson, but it was strangely quiet and there was no sign of her.

'What's that paper, Cassie?'

'Do you think we should have a look?'

Bindy nodded but felt a bit scared. Cassie reached out and moved the basket closer to them. She moved the shell, passed it to Bindy to hold, and then unfolded the note tentatively and began to read.

Dear B and C

I know you are frightened. So am I, in ways you don't yet understand. Believe me when I say I am here to help you. I am sorry I frightened you this morning. I realise now that you are true friends of M.

If you believe in me, it is important that you continue to work secretly but please trust me when I say that I am here if you need me. The work you are doing will save many people including those

*close to my heart. Thank you for your courage—you
already know that supernatural powers surround
us. Destroy this letter immediately.*

Mrs E

Bindy and Cassie stared at the letter and read it again.

'This is *so* spooky!' declared Cassie, at last, 'definitely spooky. Look at all this code stuff—B, C, E & M and she talks about the supernatural, does that mean magic?'

'Well, we know there's strange power behind the stones when they open. There's definitely mystery surrounding Morforwyn and this basket just "appearing" next to us, that's not natural, is it?' Bindy looked questioningly at Cassie who shook her head.

'No, nothing's natural at all. Pinch me, Bindy, it might all be a dream.'

'*Again*, are you sure?' Bindy duly pinched Cassie really hard on the arm.

'*Ouch*, you don't half hurt!' shouted Cassie.

'Not a dream, then!' murmured Bindy, making a cross-eyed, crazy face which made them both laugh. A much needed release of all this nervous tension and worry had caused them to feel completely exhausted and on edge. And what were they to do next?

'Do we trust her, Cassie?' Bindy asked after a little while, '*Can* we trust her?'

Cassie looked again at the letter and read,

'She says here, "The work you are doing will save many people including those close to my heart." If she's telling the truth, Bindy, and people she loves are involved then we should be able to trust her, but it's not telling us enough. I want to know who she is and *why* she's watching us. I just don't know. What do you think?'

Bindy looked at the words Mrs Easterson had written once more.

'She knows we won't betray Morforwyn, because we didn't give her away this morning. There's a lot we don't understand. She says that here. She also knows it's hard for us or she wouldn't offer her help. But she's also frightening us with all this talk of supernatural things. Is that to make us seek her help or are we walking into a trap?'

Together they sat and wondered what to do.

It was getting late, they needed to get home. Morforwyn was just down the beach but the tide was coming in and if they went now they might get trapped.

'Let's do this.' suggested Cassie. 'Let's go back home, and write a note back to Mrs Easterson asking her to tell us more, something which will prove her to be a true friend of Morforwyn. We'll put our letter in her basket and leave it at her cottage door.'

'We won't stay to speak to her, you mean?'

'No, she'll have to come to us with proof. Only then will we share any information with her.'

'Yeah, OK,' agreed Bindy, 'let's go.'

On the way up the hill, the girls reminded themselves that they needed to check out who wanted their cars washed and agreed, after tea, that they'd start visiting those nearest their own cottages. They got back to Musselshell and Mrs Hammond and Mrs Barton were in the garden playing with the swing ball. The girls looked at each other and shook their heads in disbelief, both of them thinking *'Mothers!'* The mums were having a great time, whooping with laughter each time they missed the ball, more often than not it seemed to crash into them and then they shrieked louder.

'Mum, what *are* you doing?' asked Cassie 'You're embarrassing us!'

'Oh, don't be so sensitive! Can't we have a bit of fun too? It's not everyday we get the chance!'

Cassie sighed audibly and went into the holiday home.

'It's just as well they're out there. We can get on with the writing now.'

She found a piece of paper and a pen and they went into her bedroom. They settled themselves at the dressing table and tried to think what to write.

'This isn't so easy, is it? Bindy sighed.

'No,' answered Cassie, 'but let's start anyway.' She began to think what to write.

'Um . . . . how about, *We want to trust you but need more proof. Who are you and why aren't you helping M if you think she needs it?*'

'Yes, that's sounds good,' said Bindy, so Cassie wrote the words down, then after a short pause added out loud, *'We still think you may be tricking us which is why we ask for more information.'*

They signed it. After reading it again they wondered about the last sentence. Cassie crossed out the 'tricking us' bit and wrote down something more suitable.

'That looks better, don't you think?'

'Brilliant!' agreed Bindy.

They wrote it out again on a fresh sheet of paper and read it through a second time. It now read,

> *Dear Mrs. E,*
> *We want to trust you but need more proof.*
> *Who are you and why aren't you helping M*
> *if you think she needs it?*

> *We just need a little bit more information to help us decide.*
>
> *B & C*

They threw the first sheet in the waste bin after tearing it into tiny pieces together with Mrs Easterson's letter to them. Folding the new letter carefully, they placed it in the basket and felt it was a successful note, telling her their honest feelings.

'Come on, let's sneak up to her cottage now while our mums are busy and we'll come back and have something to eat, I'm starving!'

They sneaked out while their mothers were still attempting to play swing ball in the garden and ran as fast as they could up to Kittiwake cottage. They opened the gate and walked to the door placing the basket on the mat.

'Wait!' said Bindy before they left. Her heart pounding, she took from her pocket the green shell Mrs Easterson had left on her letter and replaced it on top of their own. Cassie grabbed Bindy's hand and they ran out to the lane. They looked back briefly at the cottage and saw her at the window watching them.

CHAPTER 15

As Bindy and Cassie were having a snack with their mums in Musselshell cottage, their dads arrived home from golf. They'd had a great time, both having played well and therefore in good spirits. Having seen a bit more of the surrounding area, they suggested that they all went out for supper at a little restaurant they'd passed on the way home. It served traditional Welsh food, roast Welsh lamb, local delicacies like laverbread and cockles, cawl and other things which were quite unpronounceable but they still thought it sounded good. Everyone agreed, especially the girls, who were keen to get away tonight after the fraught time they'd had during the day. They arranged to leave at 6 o'clock. This gave the girls time to visit some cottages for their car wash enterprise.

No sooner had they finished their food they got a notebook to note down the position of the stones in each garden and what day and time was convenient to clean the cars. They also needed the car registration numbers and, more importantly, when the owners were leaving so that they could open the stones with no-one around.

After an hour, they'd discovered that all the holiday makers they'd visited were very generous in agreeing to let them clean their cars, even the three families staying an extra week. While waiting for people to open their doors, they had checked the gardens for the 'stones' and noted their positions. Later, when they looked over their list they found that they already had lots of work planned for the following day—Thursday.

There had been no sightings of Mrs Easterson, to the girls' relief, and at 4 o'clock they both felt exhausted and ready to relax before going out later with their parents. They gave each other a big, reassuring hug and went back to their own cottages.

By 6 o'clock, they were full of energy and raring to go. Bindy showered and put on her favourite dress and her mum had done her hair in a French plait. Cassie, meanwhile, had collapsed on her bed as soon as she'd got home and was now rushing to get ready as she'd fallen asleep. Mrs Barton kept calling her to hurry up and in no time at all, she'd washed, brushed her teeth, put on a skirt and t-shirt and brushed her hair frantically. It was sticking up in parts but she was past caring.

The families met on the path on the way up to the car parking area and everyone was looking forward to the night out. They were all chatting away happily and were just passing Kittiwake Cottage, when Mrs Easterson called them from her garden gate.

'*Yoo-hoo*, girls.' she called. Everyone turned and waited. Cassie and Bindy stopped suddenly, their hearts pounding in their chests.

'You left this in the shop earlier. I was just about to bring it down for you so you've saved me a journey.'

Cassie and Bindy walked back towards her, while their parents walked slowly ahead.

'I think it's yours anyway,' she said with a wink, 'Look inside,' she whispered, as she handed them a large whelk shell. Smiling and waving to their parents, she turned and went back inside the cottage.

The shell was not too large so Cassie popped it into her jacket pocket and gave Bindy a knowing look. They caught up with their parents and at the top of the hill Bindy asked her mum if she could travel with Cassie but Mrs Barton, overhearing, said,

'No need, we've got room for all of us in our car,' and so there was no chance for the girls to discover the secret contents of the shell until later. They climbed aboard the Barton's people carrier and off they went for a much needed feast. Cassie's hand curled around the shell in her pocket keeping it safe until she and Bindy had a chance to discover what was inside it.

Once they arrived at the restaurant they were greeted by a lady in Welsh costume whose name was Rhian. She turned out to be their waitress and gave them an idea of what each item on the menu was and eventually they ordered and waited for their food to come. Cassie seized the opportunity and gently kicking Bindy under the table quietly announced that she wanted to go to the loo.

'I need to go, too.' Bindy added and they leapt up from their seats and headed for the ladies toilets. Inside were four cubicles and, as luck would have it, all were free. They went into the furthest from the door and locked themselves in. Cassie pulled out the shell and looked for the message inside. There was nothing there! She'd hoped there would have been a rolled up piece of paper or something. Was Mrs Easterson tricking them?

'Well?' Bindy whispered, excitedly

'There's nothing there. Look for yourself.' Cassie handed the shell to Bindy who peered at the opening and wiggled her little finger down the hole to see if any paper had dropped further down.

'What did she say to us?' asked Bindy, still wiggling.

'She just said 'look inside' didn't she?'

'Hmm . . . O.K. so if there's nothing to pull out and read . . . . how about if we just use our eyes and actually look inside?' suggested Bindy.

'Go on then, have a look!'

Bindy placed the end of the shell to her eye and as she did so she gave a gasp.

'I can see something . . . . *Wow!*' she whispered, 'This is so weird.'

As she peered into the shell, it was as if it had become a tiny telescope through which she could see the whole undersea world opening up in front of her eyes. She could see mer-people and multi-coloured fish swimming around. Seaweeds, corals and rocks appeared and there was a figure of someone who seemed to be imprisoned. Although unclear, due to the darkness of the cave, the person, who seemed to be a man, looked so unhappy. The picture faded and a shadowy face of a young woman filled her vision. The mistiness cleared and she saw the face and heard the sweet voice of Morforwyn.

'The man you see is my father, falsely imprisoned because of evil jealousy. I am prevented from returning to the sea as I am the only one who knows the truth and my father's enemy fears I am getting closer to exposing him, so I cannot return to the sea until I can prove my father's innocence. You can help free my father. You, alone. The mystical powers involved prevent adult humans from seeking the truth or helping me

find the treasure so my mother is unable to do this for me. Very few children are untouched by the power, but you are, because you are innocent and truly believe in me and my kind of people. So many lose their belief in things they cannot see and prove. This is why you have become the ones to help. It is not by accident you discovered the stones but because of the belief you hold inside your hearts. Only you can uncover the truth. You must trust my dear brave mother. She will never betray you. Trust her completely and together we will save my father.'

There was a short silence and she then continued, *'Now show your friend what you have seen. The shell will then return to normal.'*

With a look full of wonder, she passed the amazing shell to Cassie.

'Cassie, Mrs Easterson is Morforwyn's *mother*!' she gasped.

'*WHAT?*' Cassie put the shell to her eye and Bindy watched as her friend became transfixed by what she, herself, had just witnessed.

Eventually, Cassie's hand fell away from her face. She looked bewildered by what she had seen but Bindy had recovered sufficiently to realise that they had to get back.

'Come on, Cassie, we have to go. They'll be coming to look for us otherwise!'

'Yes . . . OK . . . that was absolutely awesome!' whispered Cassie.

'Sure was!' replied Bindy. Cassie tucked the shell back into her pocket and as they came through the door, Mrs Barton came in,

'My turn now,' she smiled.

The girls walked dreamily back to their table having witnessed this strange new world through the power of the shell and were now more excited than ever to move forward with their adventure.

CHAPTER 16

Car washing day dawned dry, cloudy with some bright sunny periods, so the lady on the radio said. Cassie and her family munched through their breakfast recalling parts of the previous evening.

They'd all had a lovely time and arrived back from the restaurant quite late, singing songs all the way home, most of them making no sense, as they tried to remember choruses they'd heard. They had sat in the bar after their meal and had been treated to some live music from a traditional Welsh folk band which had everyone joining in and dancing with reckless abandon!

Cassie and Bindy had agreed to meet with their buckets and sponges at half past nine outside Musselshell Cottage and so with cheerful smiles they met up and walked together up the hill to the car park.

They had their list of registration numbers and had been told there was a tap at the parking area so carrying water wasn't a problem. With their mums' rubber gloves on they rinsed, washed, rinsed and dried two cars and realised this was not as much fun as they'd hoped! They sat down on the wooden bench tired out and in desperate need of a drink. At that moment they heard a familiar tooting horn and along came the mobile shop driven by Mrs Easterson. The girls looked at each other, then at her and she waved, giving them a really big smile. She parked, got down from the cab and came to sit beside them. The girls felt a bit nervous and kept on staring at Mrs Easterson until she said,

'My, you two look as if you've had a hard morning. How's the car washing going?'

'It's harder than we thought' replied Bindy 'and we've got another two to do before we finish today.'

'I bet you could do with a drink, couldn't you? Come into the van and I'll get you a can each.'

She opened up the back and they followed her up the steps. She told them to sit on a couple of boxes that were on the floor, then opened her fridge and produced two ice cold drinks for them which they opened eagerly.

'I'm so sorry I frightened you yesterday, will you forgive me?' she asked, looking rather concerned.

The girls stopped drinking and both nodded.

'Mrs Easterson,' began Cassie in a whisper, 'it's all so scary for us, all this magic stuff and mer-people and things and we realise you want to do all you can to help . . . 'M', but we're not sure how you *can* help when *we* have all the searching to do.'

'I know, Cassie, but this is how it must be. It's the only way my girl can help her father. Please don't give up, you are so close to finding the answers to all her problems. She has told me of her complete trust in you when she gave me the shell last night. I'll help in whatever way you can think of, by standing watch when you open the stones, perhaps, or distracting someone for you while you go to the gardens, I'm not sure how, but I want to help in whichever way you think best.' She gave them a lovely kind smile and they smiled back.

'That shell was amazing last night,' Bindy said, 'it's beautiful down there, isn't it? The sea, I mean.'

Mrs Easterson looked sad.

'Yes Bindy, it truly is a wonderful place but at the moment there is an evilness down there which is affecting the lives of so many and no-one really knows there is anything amiss. Only 'M' kno . . .' she stopped suddenly as, just then, some people entered the shop and began looking around for things they needed.

'Look, girls, why don't you call at my cottage on the way back home and I'll make you a sandwich and tell you a little more? I'll finish here at about twelve.'

She gave them a little nod of encouragement and Bindy and Cassie nodded back. They got down from the van and returned to their car washing once more. Two more and then a rest!

They worked contentedly for another hour doing an excellent job. When they were finished they called on their customers to come and inspect their work. The families turned up, examined their cars, expressed that they were very pleased with the work and happily handed over payment for a job well done. They even got extra tips and some sweets which helped their tummies considerably! The girls sat on the bench once more and felt very pleased with themselves. Four cars down, three to go.

They glanced over to the mobile shop as it was getting close to twelve o'clock and soon Mrs Easterson climbed down and locked the van door. Waving to the girls, she got her basket from the cab and walked towards them. They could smell the fresh bread rolls she had in the basket and they followed her down to Kittiwake Cottage. She lead the way into the garden and held the gate open for them to bring in all their buckets, sponges and bits and pieces and told them to leave them behind the gate. She opened the door and let them in and told them to make themselves at home while she made them something to eat.

Inside, the cottage was very homely and cosy. There were lots of bright colours in the tiny kitchen in which stood a welsh dresser filled with pretty china cups and plates and as they passed into the lounge, an old pendulum clock welcomed them with its slow, steady, tick-tock. The walls were white, but they were covered with paintings and photographs and also little wall hangings made from netting, shells and seaweed. Their eyes scanned the room looking at all the pretty things and the little wood burning stove made it a really snug place to be.

Nearly everything had a connection with the beach, even the photographs had sea, rocks or sand dunes in them and it made Cassie wonder about Mrs. Easterson being Morforwyn's mother. She was, after all, human; Morforwyn's father was a merman. How did they meet?

'Mrs Easterson, may I ask you something please, about Morforwyn's father?

'Of course, Cassie,' she replied, carrying towards them a plate of delicious looking rolls and a jug of squash. She placed them on the table with some plates and tumblers and sat down next to them. She turned towards Cassie with an enquiring look.

'What did you want to know?'

'How did you meet him?'

Mrs Easterson smiled.

'Completely by chance, I suppose' she began. 'I was living at home, not far from here, with my family. My brother was much younger, only fourteen or so at the time, and my parents were both schoolteachers. I loved being by the sea and we were always out in the fresh air whenever we had the chance.

One evening I was out walking by myself, which I often did. It was a warm evening in May and I decided to collect some mussels for our supper. I'd collected quite a few so I began to climb up the rocks and see how high I could go. It was years since I'd done any serious rock climbing and I could see a large flat rock that looked perfect for enjoying a quiet half hour of sunbathing. I reached it and lay down, albeit rather uncomfortably and closed my eyes against the brightness and warmth of the sun. However, I must have dozed off, because the next thing I knew was that it was getting dark, the tide had come back in and I was stranded on the rock.

'I could go lower but the sea was deep and I knew the current was too strong for me to swim back towards the shore. So I panicked and started shouting for help but, of course, everyone had gone home and I was alone. I looked upwards to see if I could go higher and saw that, with care, I might be able to scramble up to the top of the cliff. So abandoning my mussels, I started to climb higher but a few yards from the top I slipped and banged my back and head on the rocks below.

'I felt myself slipping and rolling down towards the sea. I was barely conscious and unable to help myself and then all of a sudden, I was in the water. I was falling into the sea deeper and deeper. I heard sounds, strange sounds, not quite music but a little like tinkling sounds echoing through my mind and I felt for certain I was going to die and I experienced a wonderful peace take hold of me but then a hand covered my nose and mouth and I felt myself being swept in another direction. I was being held by strong, confident arms and soon I began to breathe again behind the hand that covered my face.

'After a few moments I opened my eyes and saw a strange darkness, occasionally there were lights and colours but it was more of an impression than actually seeing specific things. Then I was lifted high onto a shelf of rock and a glow filled this space and I looked for the first time into the eyes of my rescuer.' She paused and looked away.

The girls waited for her to carry on. She eventually turned to them, her eyes shining. She gave a sad smile as a tear fell onto her cheek. She reached for a tissue and blew her nose.

'What a silly woman I am' she said apologetically. 'Its years ago, but I still get emotional and ridiculous!' She looked down at her hands resting in her lap, then looked up and said, 'I still feel like the young girl I was back then, I look older, but I don't feel it! I was and still am so grateful to him for saving my life, for loving me and, of course, for our beautiful daughter.'

Bindy and Cassie continued to stare at her, and felt sad. She saw their concern and smiled.

'When you're much older you'll meet lots of admirers too. I'm sure lots of boys will want to get to know you lovely girls. And one day you'll wonder whether one of them is right for you. How to choose is a big decision, one which will affect your lives in a big way. I chose against my better judgement. A merman! What a ludicrous idea! But you see he *is* a lovely man. He has an incredibly kind and gentle nature yet he has a powerful strength and such an honourable quality about him that few men would challenge him. Yes, quite an exceptional man.'

'What did he look like when you met him, Mrs Easterson?' asked Bindy.

'Oh, he was so gorgeous he literally took my breath away when I first saw him. I thought I was dreaming . . . or dead! You've heard the expression, "I thought I'd died and gone to heaven"? Well after that crack on the head, I thought I had!' She laughed happily at the girls. 'He had long, thick, wavy hair down to his shoulders, a deep golden colour. His face was very handsome, and his skin was not unlike ours, only it felt completely different. He had strong features, someone who you felt could protect you from anything and he had incredible hypnotic eyes which were deep green.

'When I had recovered sufficiently from my fall, he smiled at me, smoothed my hair, and he gazed deeply into my eyes and I was really mesmerised in the best way you can imagine. I couldn't help it, I loved him at once! I have a picture I painted of him; I'll get it for you, but it doesn't do him real justice.'

She went to a cupboard in the dresser and pulled out a large leather bound book which had a lock on it, like a diary. She took a key from around her neck, unlocked the book and flicked through the pages until she stopped at the portrait and showed them.

They looked at the face. Here, indeed, was a man of the sea, a face which was handsome but also unusual. They recognised the strength and nobility in the features but also the gentleness Mrs Easterson had described. They looked at her and smiled.

'He's really hot, I . . . I mean, gorgeous, just like you said,' smiled Cassie and went bright red.

Mrs Easterson laughed heartily at Cassie's remark

'Yes, he's special, my Kullum.' She turned more pages for them.

'These are my memories of the undersea world of merfolk, have a look and you'll see the stunning world that is down in the depths of the oceans.'

They turned the pages one by one and were quite enthralled by what they saw. One picture, however, showed Kullum with another merman. The other man had strong features too, but was very dark and also had a strange, piercing look in his eyes which was quite disconcerting.

'Who's the other man in this picture? Bindy asked

'Can't you guess?' asked their friend, sadly.

They looked again but didn't know what she meant

'That is the man who has caused all this heartache. That is Malpiddock.'

CHAPTER 17

Time was passing quickly, but the girls didn't want to stop listening to this fascinating story.

'How long did you stay down there?' they asked

'Oh well, that first day I had to let my family know I was alright, so Kullum helped me swim back to safety. He'd tended my wounds and ensured I was well enough to return after the crack on my head and we arranged to meet in a couple of days' time at the same place, near that rock, and that's how our story began and we fell in love as the summer passed. Of course, I couldn't tell my parents, they'd think I was mad! We had to meet secretly and so when I went home I had to make up stories about where I'd been. I'd spent a lot of time under the sea getting to know his family and friends and learning the ways of the merfolk.'

'How could you breathe under the sea?' asked Cassie.

'Well, that's where all the real magic comes in which I'll tell you about in a minute,'

'Wow, sounds so cool!' breathed Cassie.

'It was cool, but of course it wasn't ideal and we had to decide how our future was going to work out. We were from different worlds and our lives were completely different. So Kullum made a decision for us and came out onto land for a while and became human.'

'Gosh! How did he do that?' asked Bindy.

'Well, herein lay the heart of our problem. You see Kullum is a magician. Not as you and I understand magic but he is Chief Magician to the great sea king, Dolfo, which is an incredibly important and prestigious position in the sea king's realm. Very few merfolk possess such powerful gifts but, fortunately, Kullum was one. He was able to summon the power to change himself into a human and with those same skills was able to help me breathe easily under the sea. As I say, not all merfolk can change themselves into humans but do you know, I found out during my time under the sea that those mermaids and mermen who *can* change, often visit the human world but nobody can tell. They might seem a little strange sometimes to real humans but they manage to blend in quite easily. So, where was I? Oh yes, Kullum came to stay with me.

'He'd become human in appearance, I'd cut and styled his hair a little bit, his wonderful tail replaced by two strong legs and I took him home to meet my family. We'd woven a special story to give him credibility with my parents and luckily for the two of us they accepted him and soon grew to love him. We eventually married very quietly in the little chapel in the village and we came to live here because he needed to be close to the sea. There weren't many cottages here then, they were built later.

'I carried on working but after a while I discovered I was having a baby and had to spend a lot of time under the sea with Kullum as Morforwyn had to be born in her own environment. I was told in the beginning by Kullum that she would always be a mermaid. No human child can be born of a merman. So my pregnancy had to be a secret from my parents too and that was hard for me and very difficult having to avoid them for I loved my parents dearly and my biggest regret is that they never knew her. I spent many months between this little home and the sea and I don't know which I love most.' She smiled at the girls who stared at her open mouthed. She laughed suddenly.

'You look like a couple of fish yourselves!'

Bindy and Cassie rapidly closed their mouths and grinned at her.

'Well it's such an amazing story.' Bindy sighed, as the images that Mrs Easterson had described flooded her mind. 'So what went wrong?'

'Well, only two merfolk at that time possessed this special magical gift and, sadly, one turned his talents to evil.

'The king's Chief Magician holds office for twenty years, during which time he has to perform his tasks impeccably, then after the twenty years is up, an opportunity arises for a new challenger to take over. Now, Kullum's challenger was not prepared to wait twenty years and, jealous of his success, began to work his evil. He believed that *he* should have had the role and so this other magician, who you now know is Malpiddock, has created a lie about Kullum. It's more than that, he's created a scandal about him and, consequently, everyone believes that Kullum has betrayed and stolen from the king. The king believes it too, but it is not true because I know exactly what happened and this has been proved in the way you have become involved in this incredible mystery.'

'But if he's magic how can he not prove himself to be innocent?' asked Cassie earnestly.

'This magic is different, it's not like magic we read about in books or like the magicians we see on TV, it demands a great wisdom, kindness and purity of thought.

'This 'goodness' in turn creates vital flows of energy, which feed his power and his good reputation. It's essential in maintaining his magical skills. If merfolk hold people in high esteem, that respect creates a positive force which is channelled into the soul of the magician. The more good work the magician does for the benefit of others, the stronger his power becomes and his incredible skills increase. But once someone's honour is in doubt, the power rapidly decreases and fades and that is why Kullum is very vulnerable and unable to help himself. You saw him incarcerated below the ocean, treated like a criminal and left to die when it's Malpiddock who is the true criminal! Malpiddock's power is now getting stronger and stronger each day as he performs his magic and shows support for the king and his actions are already beginning to earn the respect of the merfolk. He has to be stopped!'

Bindy and Cassie were enthralled. They waited for Mrs Easterson to continue but she had become rather quiet and stared out of the window as it wafted in a cool breeze.

'Mrs Easterson, what did Malpiddock do to Kullum?'

'He stole the Imperial jewels belonging to the king and hid them in Kullum's cave.'

The girls let out a gasp of shock. 'Yes, such a wicked thing to do, wasn't it?' She shook her head sadly and leaned back in her chair as she continued with the story.

'When they discovered they were missing, a great search ensued and, of course, they were found where Malpiddock had placed them. Despite Kullum declaring his innocence, Malpiddock took the king to examine the royal safe and there they discovered some tail scales on the rock near the entrance where the priceless crown had been kept. After examination these were found to be Kullum's. Of course, Malpiddock had managed to obtain some scales from Kullum's tail some time previously and used them to implicate him in the 'crime'. The crown is of enormous importance to the Royal line, as you can imagine. It has been worn by the king for many, many generations and no other can ever be made as some of the metals and jewels are incredibly rare.

'The king was incensed and wanted to sentence Kullum to death but Morforwyn pleaded for his life and promised the king she knew her father was innocent and that she would clear his name. He has given her time to do this—one year. In the meantime his life remains under threat if she fails to prove his innocence.'

'How can she prove him innocent, then?' asked Bindy, 'Especially when she's on land and Malpiddock's under the sea.'

Mrs Easterson turned her head towards the girls.

'Well, her suspicions were that Malpiddock was behind the theft, because her father often told her of his jealousy and the bitter jibes Malpiddock had made at him, so this, together with the knowledge that her father would never betray the king, has taken on this task and by doing so has been able to link the imperial crown and jewels to this area and you, my dears, have already found some of that great treasure.'

'The treasure under the stones!' shouted the girls together clutching each others' hands.

'Of course!' said Cassie. 'Some of those jewels are not like anything *we've* ever seen before, that makes sense, doesn't it?'

Bindy nodded.

'The wonderful blue metal and those huge pearls!' The girls were lost in their own thoughts for a moment. Mrs Easterson watched them as they thought through this newly discovered information It was a lot for them to take in, but then Bindy asked suddenly,

'How did Morforwyn know to come here out of all the different places he could have hidden them?'

'Well this is what's so wonderful, girls,' replied Mrs Easterson with a smile. 'Morforwyn has recently discovered, due to her quest for the truth, that she possesses some of her father's power. It's not fully developed yet but she can communicate through magic, as in the shell I gave you. She has also seen visions. She saw, in dreams, the cottages on the hill, their gardens and Malpiddock chanting his spell at each stone and although these were misty uncertain visions at the time I was able to help a little with my knowledge of this area and as time has gone on, the visions are making sense because of you.' She smiled gratefully at them.

A frown clouded Cassie's face. 'But why would Malpiddock choose a place known to Morforwyn, you and Kullum. Why not choose somewhere far away in a different country where you couldn't find it? It doesn't make sense . . . . does it?'

'Well, my dears, that's where he's been very clever, don't you think? You see, he has used a place close to Kullum's heart, thereby 'proving' Kullum's guilt when they are found. Also, convincing the king and the mer-people that he stole it for the benefit of his wife, as you so cleverly pointed out, who lives here.'

'But then how will she prove his innocence even if we find all the pieces?'

Mrs Easterson looked serious for a moment and fell silent.

'That is what Morforwyn is hoping to resolve. She has no answers yet but believes that with her determination and power she will discover an error or a flaw in Malpiddock's plan which will prevent him doing any more damage, but first we have to uncover all the pieces of the royal jewels.'

CHAPTER 18

Today was the day! With plenty of luck on their side, five of the remaining jewels would be uncovered and kept safe for Morforwyn. The girls had risen very early and grabbed some breakfast explaining that they were meeting Mrs Easterson at her cottage before she had to go out. The 'story' they'd agreed to tell their parents, was that she had offered the girls a sea shell collection which she was getting rid of and they were going to have a look to decide if they wanted them. Their parents appeared to accept this.

Armed with the old shopping bag, notebook and umbrella (for hiding behind), they went on their way. Their parents had been very curious about all this paraphernalia but the girls had remained calm and non committal and mumbled something about a new game. Their dads had gone off to play golf again and their mums were going shopping and sightseeing so they didn't have to face any more awkward questions—at least, not for a couple of hours.

They had arranged with Mrs Easterson to meet up at her cottage first and it was a little past eight o'clock when they arrived there. She opened the door to let them in and they all waited until their mums passed by on their way to the car. Shortly afterwards, Mrs Easterson walked out of the cottage purposefully, armed with a wind shield to hide them, which she stuck into the lawn and stood guard by the gate while they opened the stone. She was fascinated to see the power rising from it as the girls opened it to reveal another pouch. They didn't check the contents but wrapped it inside the shopping bag and moved on to the next cottage.

Most of the holiday makers left early, taking advantage of the bright morning. As they did so, Mrs Easterson, Bindy and Cassie moved into the gardens one by one to carry out their task. Fortunately, all the gardens were quite private, having boundaries of hedges, trees and shrubs. They visited Oyster, Driftwood, Anemone and Dolphin. Identical pouches were removed and placed carefully within the shopping bag. It had all gone very well despite some passers-by stopping for a chat with Mrs Easterson, including Tom, who peered around her shoulder a couple of times as she was chatting to him, which was a bit alarming but she managed to move them all along after some small talk.

Soon all were completed and they were ready to take a break and sit down, so they made their way back up to Kittiwake Cottage and had finished well before the cleaning lady arrived to prepare the empty cottages for their next visitors. Eventually, they were back inside the cosy sitting room of Kittiwake Cottage with big smiles on their faces, feeling very pleased with themselves for a job well done. They sat down with relief and a great sense of satisfaction. Bindy and Cassie never would have managed so well without Mrs Easterson and they told her so.

'Well, girls, it's you I have to thank for being so brave and calm. It was a bit scary for me, too, you know! Of course, tomorrow, we may not be so lucky if the other families don't go out for the day. That would make things very tricky so we'll have to cross our fingers and pray for sunny weather!'

They all agreed that would be a very good idea.

'Now, let's have a cup of tea and some toast, shall we?' and off she went to the kitchen while the girls decided to look inside the bag.

Inside the first pouch they opened was a vivid turquoise coloured dolphin. It was carved from one piece of stone, the same colour turquoise that Bindy and Cassie had seen before, only this was in some ways like an opal, too. As they moved it there were different colours shining along its surface which gave the impression that the dolphin itself was moving. Its eyes were of stones of the deepest blue and the mouth was shaped by a thin line of blue metal they'd seen on the mussel shell. They placed it down on top of the pouch it had come from and reached for pouch number two.

This must have come from Oyster Cottage as it was in the shape of an oyster shell but it was the size of their hands. It was the palest coral-pink in colour. The girls handled it carefully and saw that the shade of coral increased in intensity from the outside in and every fringe of colour was edged with the most lustrous and dainty, star-shaped gems. They captured the tiniest beams of light and sparkled at every turn. Inside was beautiful pale blue mother-of-pearl lustre and locked inside this was the most beautiful blue pearl. It was breathtaking. This too was placed, once more, onto its pouch. At that moment Mrs Easterson returned with a tray of tea and toast. She placed the tray down carefully and stared, transfixed, at the two jewels that were on her table. She eased herself slowly into her chair as if a great weakness had come over her.

'Are you alright?' the girls asked her.

She looked at the beauty in front of her and spoke in a very soft broken voice,

'I never dreamed . . . . they'd look like . . . . I can't believe it.'

She sat back in her chair and looked at them again.

'I expected them to be unusual but I never imagined they would be so magnificent, they're incredibly beautiful. I never saw anything remotely like this even when I was under the sea. The jewels were never displayed and King Dolfo rarely wore his crown, only for very special occasions.' She gave a heavy sigh. 'No wonder the king was so incensed at their loss.'

'Pick them up.' suggested Bindy

'No,' replied Mrs Easterson abruptly, 'I'm afraid to touch them because Malpiddock's spell may still be on them and I cannot risk that and secondly if my fingerprints were found on them later I might jeopardise Kullum's freedom. I'll enjoy them at a safe distance. Open another one girls while I organise these drinks.'

She got up and poured the tea into three pretty cups and placed matching plates in front of Cassie and Bindy with jars of homemade jam and lemon curd. Bindy reached for the third pouch and placed it on her lap. Her hand reached in and out came an object made from flowing streams of metal wound around itself as it formed the shape. With each turn the metal changed colour, some strands were purple, some blue, some indigo, some green. As she turned it around in her hand she realised that the outline of this intertwined shape looked familiar.

'Are all the kings called Dolfo, Mrs Easterson?'

'I'm not sure,' replied Mrs Easterson. 'The royal name has been Dolfo for quite a few generations though. Why do you ask?'

'Because I think this is shaped like a D which could stand for Dolfo. Look.'

She held it up and showed them what she meant by following the shape with her finger.

'I think you could be right, Bindy' she smiled.

They sat back in their seats, not speaking a word just gazing at the treasure in front of them. After a short rest the girls discovered the contents of the other pouches, each as impressive as the last. Kittiwake's consisted of the head of a Kittiwake in profile. The head itself, made from a heavy gold coloured metal, was then somehow covered in Abalone, its eye was a clear black stone which glinted as if the eye were blinking and the strong curved beak was the same golden, shiny metal. As it was moved, the metal gleamed each time it caught the light.

Anemone Cottage produced an amazing jewel. It was, as expected, a sea anemone in shape, a smooth column carrying long fine tentacles in a rose pink coloured coral. Each tentacle, of which there were many, was tipped with bright sparkling green gems of various intensities, so delicate and graceful in design yet shimmering with bold, bright colour. Mrs Easterson had watched silently as the girls produced each priceless jewel and kept very still as they placed them one by one on the table.

The morning had been quite exhausting. All the nervous energy that had gone into this task was beginning to tell on the girls. They were feeling tired and concerned at the wealth they had in their possession. Mrs Easterson realised it was time for them to go; they still had tasks to complete before their mums came home and so they planned to meet Mrs Easterson again the following morning at half past nine. They placed the jewels in their bag.

Their next task was to wash the last three cars so they had to get back, hide the treasure and get their car washing things. It was already past 10 o'clock. As they walked through the gate they looked back at Mrs Easterson who waved from her window then they turned and walked slowly down the lane carrying the heavy bag between them. Then, from the shadow of the hedgerow, someone crept silently away.

CHAPTER 19

Their mothers had not arrived back at the cottages yet and so Bindy and Cassie called into Musselshell Cottage to collect the blue shell from Cassie's room then back at Pearl Cottage, they decided to put all the treasures into the old shopping bag in Bindy's suitcase at the back of her wardrobe. They grabbed all the buckets, sponges and soap they needed and ran up to the top of the hill to finish washing the last of the cars.

It didn't take them as long as yesterday as they were getting to be experts! By half past twelve they'd finished them all and the holiday-makers were delighted with their efforts. Even Tom had shuffled past and watched them for a while. He gave a little nod and smile for their efforts and he offered them some of his sweets.

They were pink candy shrimps which he extracted from the depths of his dusty and fluff-ridden pocket. They took one each out of politeness and told him they'd eat them later, but as soon as he'd gone they threw them into a bin, making a disgusted face at each other.

'*Huh*, I could have done with one of those, too!' Cassie complained, 'He's a bit strange, isn't he?'

'You're telling me,' replied Bindy with a snigger. 'Absolutely weird!' and she collapsed in giggles, thinking about pink, hairy shrimps.

They paused for a moment and realised, with relief that their car washing was over at last, so they took everything back to Bindy's cottage with a great feeling of satisfaction. They tidied it all away and were just getting some refreshing juice out of the fridge when Mrs Hammond walked in.

'Oh, girls, I'm really glad to see you,' she said in a concerned voice, 'have you been here all the time?'

'No, we've only just got back ourselves and we're tired out. We were just getting ourselves something to drink.'

'Why, what have you been doing that's so tiring?'

Bindy sensed something was wrong as her mother seemed rather anxious.

'You remember, Mum, washing cars and things, we told you before we went.'

'Have you washed all those cars yet?'

'Yes, we're exhausted, but in the money. We can pay you back now.'

Cassie nodded. Mrs Hammond looked at them with a very serious expression.

'Did you see Mrs Easterson? You *did* go over to her house this morning?'

'Yes, of course we did' replied Bindy, taking a long gulp of her drink.

'How long were you there?'

'From about eight o'clock until ten-ish.'

'And what were you doing from then until now?'

'Washing three cars, getting paid for it, tidying the buckets and things away and getting a drink,' answered Bindy, 'Why, Mum, what's all the panic about?'

'Girls, I'm really sorry to have to tell you . . . Mrs Easterson's been hurt . . . in an accident this morning in town, she was knocked down by a car which didn't stop.

Bindy's stomach churned and she felt tears well up in her eyes.

'Oh, no! Is she going to be OK?'

'They don't know, yet, love.'

'Where is she?'

'She's been taken to hospital. We spoke to her very briefly before the ambulance came. It happened right in front of our eyes. She'd been chatting to us about how proud we must be of you girls then she turned and stepped on to the crossing and the car seemed to come from nowhere. It hit her and sped away. Nobody managed to get a number or even identify what type of car it was. We rushed over to her but she was very confused, and mumbled something that sounded like . . . . "My poor duck". We couldn't make out what she was trying to say, it was nonsense, she must have been a bit delirious, but then she opened her eyes, looked at us and clearly said, 'tell the girls to be careful.' Then she mumbled something about 'serious danger' and 'protect them.' We've been frantic with worry which is why we rushed back home. You know that I trust you, Bindy, but what was Mrs. Easterson talking about? What were you doing? I want you both to promise that you're not doing anything silly or dangerous.'

The girls looked at each other, bewildered as to what to say and also terribly upset about Mrs Easterson.

'Well?' Mrs Hammond said, raising her eyebrows and looking at Bindy in a stern way.

Bindy was so taken aback she didn't answer immediately and felt tears well up inside her.

Cassie's chin also started to wobble. Mrs Hammond turned to Cassie and said,

'I think you'd better run home to your Mum, Cassie, and tell her you're safe and sound. She'll have got back to find you missing and will be out of her mind with worry.'

'Yes. OK. See you in a bit, Bindy.' Cassie closed the door behind her and walked briskly away.

Once out on the path, she ran towards Musselshell cottage, her mind completely in turmoil. Something alarming was going on and she began to shiver all over. She didn't believe Mrs Easterson had said 'my poor duck' at all, she knew exactly what she had been trying to say. She was saying 'Malpiddock! And if Malpiddock's power *had* caused the accident to Mrs Easterson, she and Bindy could well be in danger, too!

All she wanted at this moment was a big, reassuring hug from her mum. Of course, when she came face to face with her mother she got a serious telling off and this was just about more than she could take. While her mum was still in full flow, Cassie burst into uncontrollable tears which then made her mother look rather less angry and more anxious. She walked up to her daughter and put an arm around her shoulders.

'Look Cassie, I'm only worried for your safety. I'm sorry I was feeling so cross but you're very precious, you know, and young girls like you and Bindy need to be very careful, especially in a strange place. You don't usually keep things from us. It's very worrying.'

She wrapped Cassie in her arms and gave her a great big cuddle. This made Cassie cry even harder and soon she was sobbing uncontrollably.

Her mother tilted her chin towards her and asked,

'Cassie, I can tell there's something more to this. Please tell me if you're in trouble or if there's something bothering or frightening you.'

Cassie blinked up at her mother's kind face and thought about what she should say. She really wanted to tell her everything. Now may be the right time. Should she talk to Bindy first?

'Come on, sweetheart,' her mother urged,' tell me what's worrying you.'

Her mum always made her worries go away and she so wanted to feel safe and happy instead of miserable and frightened.

'I want to tell you mum, I really do, but I can't. As soon as I can I will, I promise. Please don't ask me any more. I'm OK, really I am, but first I've got to go and see Bindy.'

'Now listen to me, Cassie,' Mrs Barton replied firmly, 'you can't keep important secrets from me or your dad and you're going to have to promise to tell us everything as soon as your father comes home.'

Cassie's heart sank. Everything was going wrong. This was not the way things were meant to happen.

'Oh no.' she thought, 'what's Bindy going to say!'

'Mum, I promise I'll tell you. Please don't worry, but Bindy and I have to talk first.' She ran out of the cottage and back to Bindy's. As she was about to knock on the door, Bindy came rushing out and before Cassie could make her confession, Bindy herself whispered frantically,

'Oh, Cassie, I've done something terrible!'

'What have you done?'

'I've told my mum about Morforwyn!'

Cassie grabbed Bindy's arm and dragged her into the garden.

'What! How much have you told her?'

'Well, she asked me to explain what Mrs Easterson meant. So I told her that we were trying to help someone else in trouble. She asked who it was and when I didn't answer she ordered me to tell her who it was or else I was to stop seeing you for the rest of the holiday. So I said 'Morforwyn' then she asked me who Morforwyn was . . . . so I said . . . . a mermaid!' Bindy looked down at her feet feeling completely miserable. She felt she'd betrayed Morforwyn and Cassie.

'Did she believe you?' asked Cassie.

'She just said *'A mermaid?',* in that completely disbelieving way parents have when they think you're lying, she stared at me as if I was crazy and I'm sure she thinks I've gone potty!'

'Well, she obviously thinks you're making up this far-fetched story to avoid telling her the truth. I mean, you've got to admit, it's a pretty mind-boggling excuse you've given her. She's bound to think you're lying. The trouble is she probably thinks you're covering for me. There's no-one else here who knows you. The only down side of this is that they probably won't let us stay friends now. Oh, knickers!' she groaned. 'And that's not all.'

'Why, what else can go wrong?' asked Bindy

'I came over to tell you that I did almost the same thing with Mum.'

Bindy looked up, almost grateful that she wasn't the only one to succumb to the strain of it all.

'What did you tell her?'

'Well, before I said anything she went absolutely bonkers thinking I was in danger and wanted to know if I was hiding something. She kept asking me to tell her what was going on. I said I couldn't tell her until I'd spoken to you. I told her not to worry, so she said I had to tell them both tonight exactly what was going on!'

'We're going to have to come clean, Cassie,' said Bindy, then her shoulders sagged a little, thinking about the accident. ' . . . and poor Mrs. Easterson!'

'Yeah, I know. By the way, you know what she was trying to say, don't you?'

'What?'

'When your mum thought she said "my poor duck"?'

'No. What?'

'I think she was saying 'Malpiddock!'

They stared at each other, both of them realising that if Malpiddock's power could hurt Mrs Easterson he was really close.

'If our parents think we can't be trusted,' continued Cassie, 'then our work in saving Kullum has been useless. We have to convince them that Morforwyn exists without seeing her and that Malpiddock is real. There is only one thing we can do before facing our parents and that is to get the best help available.' She grabbed Bindy's arm and pulled her towards the gate. 'We've got to see Morforwyn and get her to help before we tell our parents anything! Come on, let's go to see her now.'

'Have you got your shell?' asked Bindy.

Cassie searched in her jeans pocket and pulled out the green shell Morforwyn had given her.

'And I've got mine. Come on!'

As they ran down the hill Mrs Hammond shouted after them to come back. She wasn't sure if they'd heard or not and sighed in frustration at the two disappearing figures.

'For goodness' sake, *now* where are they going!' she cried in exasperation.

CHAPTER 20

Bindy pulled Cassie up the rocky shelf to Morforwyn's cave. They settled themselves comfortably as they pulled out their shells but before they called her name they heard a cry. It sounded like a lament, her voice clear but mournful, which echoed through the cave. They placed the shells in the palm of their hands and whispered, 'Morforwyn' and the sound stopped. Again, they heard the familiar shuffling, moving slowly, this time, towards the mouth of the cave. When she appeared she looked pale and unwell.

'Morforwyn, are you alright?' asked Bindy

'Yes, I am well but I am anxious also, for news. I feel deep sadness inside me and sense something is wrong. I fear my father is growing very weak. Something has happened and I feel sorrow here.' She placed her hand over her heart. 'What can you tell me?'

'Oh, Morforwyn, everything's going wrong.'

'Why, what has happened? Have you been able to find the treasure?'

'Yes, at least we've got seven pieces, three left to do tomorrow morning. But Mrs Easterson, who's been helping us release the treasure, has had a terrible accident.'

They told Morforwyn the details of what happened. Morforwyn looked very anxious when they spoke of Mrs Easterson being in hospital. She held her face in her hands and shook her head despairingly, whispering *'Mother, Mother.'*

Despite her distress, they felt they had to press on.

'The only problem is that our parents are convinced we've done something terrible, that we're in danger and so they want us to tell them everything tonight. Bindy's even told her mum about you being a mermaid but, of course, she doesn't believe her. We've rushed down here to ask your advice. What can we say to them?'

Morforwyn looked at them and they could tell she was thinking hard. Then she spoke.

'Malpiddock's power is clearly reaching out from the sea. My mother recognised this immediately and wanted to warn you. Something she saw made her certain of this, though what it could be, I'm not sure. Each time the treasure's released out of his power, his spell is broken so he must be weakening and is fighting back with his wickedness. But by doing evil he risks his reputation and ultimately his influence will weaken. What he did today will have lost him a great deal of power. He stopped my mother because he feels you are close to revealing the truth. Despite her being harmed, this is temporary, I am certain she will recover, for if he kills her he is guilty of murder and risks his status, his position and his power. So what happened today gives me hope. He is losing his composure; he will begin to make mistakes. We are close to the truth and he knows it.' She placed her hands over her eyes for a while and they waited. After some minutes she said,

'Yes, I sense him now, he is angry, disturbed. You must continue to recover the jewels. Everything rests on these.'

She smiled at them and saw something else was on their minds

'Tell me what bothers you.'

'Well, as we said, we have these three stones to uncover but with Mrs Easterson in hospital we're on our own again and we still don't know what to tell our parents. If we don't give them a satisfactory explanation they won't let us stay friends, we won't be able to recover the other treasures and everything will go wrong!'

'I see.' She played with some shells that were threaded onto a bracelet on her wrist. In due course she looked up at the girls who were waiting anxiously.

'You must tell them the truth. You must go home and show them the seven jewels. You must show them all to your parents tonight and they will recognise that they are not from the human world. These gems are only found in the greatest depths of the oceans. Then you must ask them to take you to visit my mother in hospital. Wait a moment.'

She turned away from them and went into her cave. Some moments later she returned holding a large stone bowl and hanging over the edges were what seemed to be different types of sea plants. She placed it down on the rock, picked up a smooth pebble and pounded the contents until it was pulp. Then from her waist she took a small pouch. It appeared to be the same type of leather as the jewel pouches and it looked as if it might be the skin of a sea mammal.

'Inside this bag is special medicine.' She took out a pinch or two of the powdery substance and added it to the pulp. She then took a mussel shell and scooped the mixture into a deep shell covering it with a layer of seaweed to keep it moist. 'When you and your parents are alone with my mother, spread this remedy on her brow and leave it there.' She then handed them a small, purple-black crystal. 'Take this, it has reviving properties, and place it in her hand. Within a few moments she will be strengthened and will be able to speak clearly to your parents. She may even remember what it was she noticed, but no matter if she doesn't. What's important is that she supports your story.'

'I'm not sure this will work.' Bindy sighed. 'I've already said you're a mermaid and my mother thought I was crazy!'

'You will find the right words, have faith in yourselves and believe what you're doing is right and your parents will see that you are genuine. Most importantly, be tranquil, confident, don't lose your patience. You have no reason to be afraid; you've already proved your courage.'

She smiled warmly at them.

'Hurry now, my dear friends, and don't give up. I'll see you here tomorrow as soon as all the jewels have been collected. I'll be waiting.'

The girls said goodbye and began climbing back down onto the sand.

As they looked up the beach they saw Mrs Hammond coming towards them with Trilby.

'*Oh-oh*' sighed Bindy in a low voice, 'Here comes trouble!'

They walked silently up to Mrs Hammond who had let Trilby off his lead. He was busy digging a hole in the sand and quite oblivious of everyone else. They did not hide what they held in their hands and so when she reached them Mrs Hammond asked,

'What have you got there?'

'It's something for Mrs Easterson, to make her better.' Bindy replied.

'What is it?'

'Morforwyn has made up a special remedy which she wants us to take to her tonight.'

Mrs Hammond looked sceptically at her daughter, but Bindy held her gaze, her eyes clear and holding no trace of pretence.

'Show it to me, please.' Her mother insisted.

Bindy turned over the seaweed cover and showed the mixture that had been prepared.

'We have strict instructions about what to do with it.' Cassie added, looking seriously at Mrs Hammond.

She in turn looked back at them and without a word tried to put a finger out to touch the pulpy mixture. Bindy instinctively swerved the shell and its contents away from her.

'Sorry, Mum, but this is especially for Mrs Easterson, even we haven't touched it. It will help her explain to you what's going on.'

Her mother looked quite infuriated then looked up to the rocky ledge where they'd met Morforwyn.

'Is she there now?' she asked.

'Of course.' Bindy answered.

'Will you introduce me?' her mum asked in a rather casual way.

The girls looked at each other for a few moments. Cassie took out her shell

'I could go and ask her, if you like?' she offered.

Bindy shrugged and thought *'why not?'*

119

'OK, I'll wait here with Mum.' They stood in silence watching Cassie run back to the rocks and climb up to Morforwyn's cave. After some minutes, they saw her emerge. She stood upright and beckoned them to come forward.

Bindy and her Mum walked steadily towards the rock, and then climbed up until they were next to Cassie.

'Morforwyn thinks it is a good idea to meet your mum. She's inside the cave and wants us all to go inside.'

'Really?' Bindy whispered, surprised at this development.

Mrs Hammond took this to be a game that the girls were playing with her.

'Oh, this I must see!' she laughed and walked inside.

CHAPTER 21

Mrs Hammond walked confidently inside the cave but after a few steps had to stoop to avoid bumping her head. It was dark and it took a while for her eyes to become accustomed to the dim interior. She blinked a few times and then her eyes caught sight of a glow right at the back of the deep cave. Crouching down underneath a shelf of rock to reach the light she began to make out a shadowy figure in the distance. This took her by surprise as she had not expected there to be anyone inside at all, believing that the girls were tricking her. She was conscious of them following quietly behind her and so took a few more steps forward. As she tried to straighten, she suddenly gasped as something damp brushed against her face and, as she did so, she heard a gentle musical voice speak to her from the shadows.

'Don't be afraid, I will not harm you.'

They continued to walk deeper and deeper into the cave until they began to make out a vague outline then, with an unexpected flick of her arm, a bright light glowed around the rocks on which Morforwyn sat and all three humans suddenly gasped and stared at the magnificence of the beautiful mermaid, clearly at home in her cavernous surroundings. Her hair fell in waves over her shoulders, over which she wore a bodice of fine woven seaweeds threaded with abalone shells and tiny pearls. Her hands were outstretched in welcome and, in all its glory, her splendid silvery-blue tail curled and swished against the damp floor of the cave.

'Come,' she whispered, 'come and sit closer.'

Mrs Hammond turned and looked at the girls.

'. . . B-b-b-but . . . . I . . . . b-b-but . . . . '

'Come on Mum, it's OK, I promise.' Taking her mother's hand in hers, she realised that she was shaking, which surprised her, as she thought only children felt nervous like that. Her mother allowed herself to be dragged closer and closer to Morforwyn who indicated another rock on which Mrs Hammond could sit. She lowered herself onto it and at the same time felt the cold dampness seep into her clothes. She looked at the beautiful creature with some trepidation and waited.

'Are you comfortable there?' she asked Mrs Hammond.

'Yes . . . . thank you,' she replied, hesitantly, clutching Trilby's lead tightly in her hands.

'I appear to have shocked you, I am so sorry.' She reached out and touched Mrs Hammond on the hand. She felt the strange, cold, dampness touch her skin which left a tingling sensation.

'Young people like Bindy and Cassie find it easy to accept that there are unusual life forms on this earth because they want to believe it so very much. But as humans grow older, and supposedly wiser, they lose that passionate belief in things, they become self-righteous and lose the wonderful, innocent, passion for things they can't explain. They keep needing evidence, confirmation, and verification. Although, you know, deep inside their hearts they really want to believe in what they can't see. Their minds tell them that others will think them foolish so they dismiss it as only make-believe, myth, legend and fairy tale.' She looked directly into Mrs Hammond's eyes.

'Now that you see me and feel my touch, you know it's not any of those things. It's truth, certainty, life. A different life from yours, of course, but nevertheless a wonderful, fascinating life. Bindy and Cassie believed without asking me for proof. That's what makes them special and today is the very first time they've seen all of me. As you can see, I am Morforwyn, undeniably of the sea.' She gave them a proud smile and a big flick of her wonderful tail that sent the hair on their heads waving in its draught. She looked serious again.

'You may wonder why I've risked inviting you to see me. I am aware of the danger I could face if you betray me, but knowing your daughter, as I do, I believe I can trust you.

'It's very important that you believe everything they have to tell you tonight so please do everything they ask of you. Believe in them, they are very courageous children. They are here because they are ready to help an innocent stranger. Be proud of them and give them all the support they need. Now I must go and so must you.'

Mrs Hammond found her voice and looked back at the beautiful creature.

'But Mrs Easterson talked about danger. Are you placing them in serious danger? I need to know, as a mother, before I agree to help.'

Morforwyn looked her straight in the eyes, and Mrs Hammond felt a chill running down her spine.

She whispered in a low voice,

'They are only in danger if you fail them.'

She leaned back, her arms stretched above her head and seemed to rise with ease as she leapt backwards into a dive, her body twisting in the air. They watched as her tail disappeared behind the rock and soon a gentle splash was heard as she entered the deep water below.

The cave had returned to an eerie darkness, they could only hear the faint drips of water falling on the floor of the cave and the beating of their own hearts. Mrs Hammond rose slowly from her rock and immediately felt the dampness on the back of her trousers.

'*Ugh!* I'm all wet! Let's get out of here!'

She moved quickly and eventually walked out into the open air. She stood still, took a deep breath, then another and another. Bindy and Cassie watched but said nothing, waiting for her to speak, but she remained absolutely silent. They followed her as she climbed down onto the sand. Trilby was lying there with a completely chewed stick in shreds close to his nose. He wagged his tail at the sight of them and sat up. Mrs Hammond held him by his collar and attached his lead. Bindy and Cassie didn't like the silence that hung over them and began to feel a sense of foreboding. Was Mrs Hammond going to betray Morforwyn? Did she believe her? Will this have made any difference or will it have made her even more determined to put an end to their quest? The silence continued all the way up to Pearl Cottage.

At their gate Mrs Hammond turned and spoke to Cassie.

'Cassie, I want you to go home now and tell your parents to come over to us here at . . .' she looked at her watch, did a bit of mental calculation and continued,' . . . half past three. Your dads will have had time to settle down before we all get together and talk this thing through.

'Don't tell them anything yet about what we've just seen, but your mother will need to tell your father about what happened to Mrs Easterson and what she said, OK?' She laid a hand gently on Cassie's shoulder and Cassie nodded in response.

Mrs Hammond told Bindy to take Trilby inside while she stayed in the lane watching Cassie safely back into Musselshell Cottage then she turned around and walked thoughtfully back to her own cottage.

CHAPTER 22

At half past four that afternoon, the two families were sitting in the small lounge of Pearl Cottage listening intently as the story of Morforwyn and her father unfolded. The girls told them about how they discovered Morforwyn; how they crept out in the middle of the night and the power they felt as the stones were opened. Mr Hammond was very annoyed that they'd been so foolhardy and reckless and was not too happy that they'd deceived him into thinking that Bindy was asleep when, in fact, she'd been outside the window! They told them about the shells which they used to summon Morforwyn, about Mrs Easterson's life and how she met Kullum and that she was Morforwyn's mother. Their parents' reaction to this was one of complete disbelief and scores of questions were put to the girls but they calmly answered all of them and by so doing their parents began to accept a little bit more of the story. Eventually, more normal conversation resumed. Cassie and Bindy took them outside to the cottage nameplate and demonstrated how the pearl came out and then opened the stone once more. This time the power was dead.

There were many interruptions and questions and at one point their fathers, in turn, began to raise their voices against any further involvement by the girls. They would not accept the strange goings on and refused to allow the girls to talk any more about it.

At this point the girls were exhausted and began to feel the dread of failure; this was not going to go any further. They'd done their best but they were up against two stubborn fathers who had forgotten what it was like to believe. Morforwyn was right, they were too set in their ways to change and the girls began to feel completely dejected.

Mrs Hammond gently told the girls to get the bag. They'd forgotten to show them the treasure! While they fetched it, Mrs Hammond spoke for the first time about her experience in the cave earlier that day. As the grown-ups realised she had actually met the mermaid a stunned silence hung in the room. Her husband looked at her in astonishment and told her she must be barmy! She acknowledged to them her own scepticism on the beach as the girls tried to convince her of Morforwyn's existence. This was before she'd entered the cave. But since she had come face to face with this real, live mermaid, she described how, in her heart, she could relate to the insistent way Morforwyn spoke to her which, after listening to the whole story, left her in no doubt that what they were being asked to do was the right thing. She expressed the importance of the work Bindy and Cassie had been chosen to do. She then announced that if no-one else helped their brave girls, she'd have to do it by herself.

Cassie and Bindy had no idea how Mrs Hammond had felt earlier in that cave and Bindy's heart filled with a great wave of pride for her mother and felt tightness burn in her throat as sobs grew inside her. It was no good trying to hold them back because her heart was so full of love and gratitude. She cried and ran into her arms. Cassie, overcome with relief, cried too and ran to Bindy and Mrs Hammond. The sight of her holding these two sobbing girls made everyone realise that this, indeed, was something momentous. The two dads looked at each other, shaking their heads in disbelief, while Mrs Barton strode over to her daughter, took her in her arms and whispered, 'OK, you win!'

After much hugging, blowing noses and making cups of tea, the bag was opened and for the first time the adults saw the unbelievable beauty of the treasure uncovered so far. The girls explained that they were not to touch them but they brought each one out to show them their exquisite beauty. They were all entranced. Bindy and Cassie wrapped them up carefully, replaced them in the bag and returned them to the safety of Bindy's room.

While they were away, and their wives were washing the dishes, Mr Barton rubbed his hands over his eyes and said,

'I hope we're doing the right thing, here.'

'Hmm,' replied Mr. Hammond, 'the trouble is these women are so ready to jump into danger. They don't seem to realise that if any of this goes pear—shaped, it's *us* poor devils will have to stand up against the mad magician!'

'Oh Lord, don't even think about it!' sighed Mr Barton.

'Think about what?' asked Mrs Barton coming back into the lounge.

'Think it's time to go to the hospital, dear.' He smiled, winking at Mr Hammond who rose from his chair, clapped him on the back and shouted,

'Come on, girls, time to go!

Hospital visiting was from seven until eight o'clock. The mums enquired which ward Mrs Easterson was in and they were told Ward 11. They bought some flowers and a card and hurriedly wrote it before finding the lift to the second floor.

Ward 11 was a busy bustling ward, with all the beds occupied mostly by people who had arms, necks or legs strapped up. Most had visitors chatting to them and lovely vases of flowers beside their beds or 'Get Well' balloons floating close to the ceiling. Eventually they caught sight of Mrs Easterson who lay very still, with a bandaged head, in the corner of one of the rooms.

Bindy and Cassie had brought the mixture but there was no privacy and they weren't sure how they would carry out Morforwyn's instructions.

Mrs Barton drew up a chair next to her and gently called,

'Mrs Easterson?' but there was no response. 'Mrs Easterson, the girls have come to see you. They've brought you something from your daughter.'

Her eyes gave a little flicker and then closed again.

Mrs Hammond went out to speak to one of the nursing staff. The only person she found was a young auxiliary nurse busily searching for something she clearly couldn't find.

'I'm sorry to interrupt, but I wonder if you could tell me whether Mrs Easterson has been awake at all this evening, please?'

The staff member continued to hunt, and responded to Mrs Hammond while her head was still bent down looking through some files in a drawer.

'Not much, I'm afraid, she's still very weak. Don't stay too long, she needs plenty of rest.' she mumbled as she continued her search.

When she returned to the bedside, Mrs Hammond took hold of the privacy curtain and pulled it around the bed.

'There's no-one around,' she said, 'apart from an auxiliary and she's too busy to notice anything, so let's get on with it.' She gave the girls a little nod and they quickly spread the mixture onto Mrs Easterson's forehead, being careful not to move the bandage then Cassie took out the crystal and placed it gently in Mrs Easterson's hand. They waited. After a matter of two to three minutes, her skin began to absorb the mixture and after a little while it had completely gone. The girls watched their parents' reaction—they looked completely bewildered, but said nothing. Just at that moment, Mrs Easterson opened her eyes, blinked a few times and recognised that she had visitors. She sat herself up against her pillows.

'Oh my dear girls, there's lovely to see you!' she smiled and reached out to touch their hands. She patted them both gently.

'What have I got here?' she said frowning and looked at the object in her other hand 'Oh, you've been to see Morforwyn!' she whispered.

'Yes, she gave us the mixture to put on your forehead and told us to give you this to hold. It worked, just like she said it would!' smiled Bindy.

'Well, of course! You didn't really expect it not to, did you?' she smiled. She touched her forehead gently and said, 'I can't feel anything.'

'No, it's gone into your skin.'

'Good gracious! Marvellous medicines they have, you know. I'm feeling as right as rain!' She smiled at the girls and slowly realised that their parents were sitting there listening.

'It's lovely to have all these visitors. To what do I owe all this attention?'

Mrs Hammond sat close to her on the bed and took her hand.

'Well, in addition to wanting to see how you are, we've been ordered to come by those two young ladies over there.' She smiled towards Bindy and Cassie. 'I thought you'd also like to know that I've seen and spoken to Morforwyn and we're all ready to take over in helping the girls while you rest in hospital.'

'Well isn't that marvellous! Girls, you must be very proud of your wonderful parents.'

'Yes, we are,' they both choroused, 'we thought they'd never believe us but they've been amazing.'

Both Mr and Mrs Barton and the Hammonds looked very pleased with themselves and grinned back at Mrs Easterson.

'Well that's good.' She sat herself straighter and faced the grown ups. 'You know most of the story by now I expect, but even though you think you might know better, you have to listen to what the girls tell you to do. That will not seem fitting to you initially but don't forget that, being innocent children, they are well protected whereas you might pose a danger to them by taking control over . . .' she lowered her voice, ' . . . *Malpiddock*. It will mean a bit of role reversal for you, I'm afraid, but that's the only way we can keep everyone safe. Now do you have any questions?'

Mr Barton cleared his throat gently,

'Mrs Easterson, we still feel uneasy and have many concerns about the danger you spoke of after your accident, what was it you saw that made you realise that danger? Do you remember yet?'

'Oh, the accident.' she pondered a little then exclaimed 'Yes, I do remember now! As I turned to cross the road. I looked at the traffic, as you do, and as the driver came towards me I saw a very strange look on his face, as if he was aiming for me and, in that split second as he hit me, I realised it was Malpiddock's face behind that wheel. Now, whether he has come on land and become human or whether he has merely used his power to make it look as if he was driving, I really don't know. Anything is possible where he is concerned! So the only thing I can reassure you about is that you must remember two very important things. The first is that as he continues to do evil his power diminishes. Secondly, he cannot overpower innocence and purity so the girls are your main weapon against him.'

'But his power will only diminish if merpeople discover his evil deeds, isn't that so? How can we, as humans, discredit him?' asked Mr Barton.

'Well, I believe he *does* lose some power by doing evil however you're quite right in that the most damaging thing to him is the lack of respect by his own people. The only answer is to lead him to Morforwyn, I suppose. And once she has the proof, he is lost.'

CHAPTER 23

The journey back was a fascinating mixture of excitement and serious planning, especially as they were all supposed to be leaving on Saturday. The Barton's offered to contact the agents the following morning to see if they could all stay on one more night. They agreed that Mr and Mrs Hammond should be the 'look-outs' while the girls uncovered the stones in the last three gardens. At least it would look more natural to have two people chatting on the lane in case anyone wondered what the girls were doing.

Having had an exciting and very tiring day, everyone fell into bed exhausted but back in her deep, dark, pool, below her cave, Morforwyn began to contemplate how she would overcome the powers of Malpiddock if and when she had to face him tomorrow.

At around 9 o'clock the Hammonds called on the Bartons to collect Cassie. They felt it would be a good idea to move into the gardens as soon as the families left so they had to take turns in keeping an eye on activities in the lane. Eventually, Coral Cottage's elderly couple left for a walk. Having borrowed the wind break from Mrs Easterson's garden, Mr and Mrs Hammond, with the large, heavy, treasure bag joined the girls.

Bindy and Cassie felt so much calmer that they were coming to the end of their task, however their parents could not disguise that they were rather nervous as to what might happen as a result. Nevertheless, they arrived at Coral Cottage, whose stone was to the side of it. They would be well hidden from sight. They removed the coral 'key' from the nameplate with a bit of a struggle and disappeared around the corner to open the stone. Just as before, it sprang open with a rich, pink glow and inside they found another pouch which they tucked into a pocket, closed the stone and returned, with windbreak, to the front of the cottage. While Bindy placed the pouch in the treasure bag, Cassie replaced the coral key and waited until they could move to the next cottage. After a little while, the inhabitants of Lobster Cottage moved off.

Their task was a little trickier here as the key was very stiff and wouldn't come out of the nameplate easily. It was such an awkward shape, the girls couldn't get a good enough grip and then a group of walkers passed. One stopped to admire the view and kept chatting to the Hammonds so the girls had to pause until they went past. No sooner had they gone than Tom ambled up the lane and had a good look into the garden as the girls were still trying to wiggle away at the key. He nodded to Bindy's Dad, then stopped, turned around, possibly forgetting which way he was going, and went back towards the beach again. Bindy and Cassie waited a few seconds then hissed at Mr Hammond to come and help, so while the coast was clear, he ran quickly towards the door and tried to move the key. Luckily, his strength loosened it and Bindy took over. At last the key was free! The stone was close to the lane, behind the hedge, so they had to work quickly before anyone else passed. The stone opened just as fiercely as before and accompanied by the same colourful glow, they retrieved the pouch of treasure. Quickly, they leaned over the hedge, popped it straight into the bag and returned the stone and key.

'*Phew!*' sighed Cassie 'I'll be glad when they're all finished, won't you?'

'Absolutely!' answered the three Hammonds in unison. They walked back to Musselshell Cottage and waited outside as they'd arranged to meet up with the Bartons at ten o'clock. It was just five minutes past ten but there was no sign of them.

'I wonder if they're ready,' said Mr Hammond, 'Cassie, do you want to give them a shout while we wait by Pearl Cottage and then we can all go to Island Cottage together before we leave for the beach?'

'OK,' she replied, opening the gate, 'see you in a bit.' Suddenly, the weather changed and rain started to fall. Cassie opened the door of her cottage and called out to her parents, but there was no reply. The cats were sleeping on the sofa so she gave them a quick smooth before looking in the bedroom. No, nobody in there either.

'*MUM! DAD!*' she shouted, running back out into the garden. Then she noticed the stone was open and felt her heart skip a beat. She suddenly felt cold. Something bad was happening. She didn't know quite what it was, but she knew her parents were in danger. They would never have left this morning, never!

She ran out to the lane, tears coursing down her cheeks, calling frantically to the Hammonds. They turned and saw Cassie shouting in panic.

'They're not there! The stone's been opened again and there's no sign of them!'

Bindy ran into her own garden.

'Oh no! Look, our stone's open too! What's happening?'

Mr Hammond looked bleak and said,

'I think Malpiddock's here. We've got to act quickly and get to Island Cottage before he does! Come on!'

The rain fell more heavily but, oblivious to the weather, they all ran as fast as they could down to Island Cottage. They dashed to the doorway, removed the Island key and looked around for the stone. Mrs Hammond looked through the windows to see if anyone was at home but it seemed empty. Cassie remembered the stone was behind the cottage in front of some tall bushes. The others all followed her and stayed together while the girls checked it. It was still untouched. They immediately set to work. The stone shot open and despite being a bright sunny day, the lights that poured from the ground were as bright as fireworks, they shot up to the sky. They all stood back in astonishment. Bindy and Cassie looked into the ground and instead of a pouch being there they saw a very large box. It was carved with all types of sealife and was cold to the touch. Bindy reached in to lift it out but it was too heavy to move.

'Help me, Cassie!'

Cassie bent lower and took hold of the other end but again it was too heavy for them. Then, suddenly, they heard a rustling in the bushes. They staggered back unsure what was going to appear and out came Tom, not quiet and ordinary anymore but strong and intimidating. He looked at them

'I'll take that.' he said pushing the girls out of the way. He closed his hands around the box, lifted it out and said gruffly, 'Follow me.'

'Wait one moment' said Mr Hammond in a strong voice.

Tom walked towards him and put his face inches from Mr Hammond's.

'If you want to see the Bartons again, do as I say. NOW!'

Cassie almost crumpled. Mrs Hammond put a reassuring arm around her and whispered,

'Come on. They'll be alright but we have to do what he says. Just remember what you've been told.'

They all followed Tom down to the beach. Each of them trying to remember everything Mrs Easterson had said to them the previous night; *The most damaging to him is the lack of respect by his own people . . . . Lead him to Morforwyn . . . . once she has the proof, he is lost . . . . He cannot overpower innocence . . . . the girls are your main weapon against him.'*

The beach was empty, unusually so, despite the sudden change in the weather. There was no-one around at all. No seagulls calling, no children shouting or laughing. Even the sea was still. But the clouds were dark and the atmosphere was full of tension.

Tom strode on carrying the heavy box in his arms. He was walking towards Morforwyn's cave. He knew exactly where she was. He stopped abruptly and looked at Bindy and Cassie.

'Now, you two go into the cave and call on your friend.' he said in a stern tone.

'We want that box first.' said Bindy defiantly.

'DON'T ARGUE WITH ME, GIRL!' he bellowed.

'Don't speak to my daughter like that!' Mr Hammond shouted back, holding Tom by the sleeve. He shook himself free of Mr Hammond's grasp and bent towards him menacingly.

'I've told you once, if you don't get your daughter to listen to me, we are all lost.'

Mr Hammond looked at him perplexedly. He turned to the girls and said,

'Do what he says.'

'WAIT!' Tom shouted.

He took the heavy treasure bag from Mr Hammond and gave it to the girls.

'Take this with you,' he said gruffly. Surprised by this order, the girls took hold of a handle each and, despite its weight, began to climb up the wet jagged rocks towards Morforwyn's cave. Up and up they went as quickly as they could with the precious bag which became heavier with every step.

Back on the sand below, with water lapping at their feet, Tom walked around to the back of the rock followed by the Hammonds and there, gagged and tied with some strange, strong binding were the Bartons. Mrs Barton tried to make a sound but the gag was too tight. Her husband looked helpless despite trying to release himself. Mr and Mrs Hammond stared at the sight and shouted at Tom to release them.

'QUIET! The tide will be in soon and unless you do exactly as I say, I cannot be held responsible for their safety.'

'You evil scoundrel!' shouted Mr Hammond.

'You're a madman!' screamed Mrs Hammond launching herself at him.

'STAND BACK!' he shouted, 'You know nothing of what's going on here. I'm showing you what might happen to them if you try to do something stupid. Now follow me. We haven't a moment to lose.'

He walked back around the rock and began to climb up to the cave. The Hammonds followed wondering what he was going to do. In their minds they kept thinking about the girls. '*They are your best weapon . . . they are your best weapon . . .* '

CHAPTER 24

Bindy and Cassie had whispered Morforwyn's name into their shells and were inside the cave. They heard Morforwyn very faintly from deep inside so began moving slowly towards the place they'd found her the day before, carefully manoeuvring underneath the low rocks.

'Come on girls, come in. Bring the bag with you.' It was as dark as it had been yesterday but they couldn't make out Morforwyn at all.

'This way, keep walking towards me.' They heard a shuffling sound and began to move closer realising they were now able to stand upright, so they had to be getting closer.

'We can't see properly,' said Bindy, 'please give us some light, Morforwyn, It's scary in here.'

'Come closer and I'll light your way. Did you gather all the jewels?'

'Yes, we've got them here. At least . . . .' Cassie began.

'At least, what?' demanded Morforwyn in a sharp voice.

This didn't sound like the Morforwyn they knew. They stopped momentarily and took hold of each other.

'That doesn't sound like Morforwyn to me.' whispered Bindy.

'Something's wrong!' Cassie said quietly to Bindy, 'Stay with me, whatever you do.' She shouted out 'We're not coming any closer until we see you, Morforwyn, give us light.'

There was a long pause, and then, suddenly, the cave flooded with light. They screamed in terror for the creature that stood in front of them was not Morforwyn but a large menacing figure. His head almost touched the ceiling of the cave, his tail coiled like a snake beneath him, his body, scaly and strong bent over them threateningly, with evil alive in his face. They knew instinctively who this was—Malpiddock! *THIS* was Malpiddock!

Bindy and Cassie clung to each other and both could feel the other trembling. He saw their discomfort and let out a laugh which was loud and frenzied but which turned into a snarl.

'You fools, you poor, misguided fools! Nobody can challenge *ME!* Innocent children—Ha! They don't understand just how powerful I am! *GIVE ME THAT BAG!'*

The girls took a few steps back. Cassie let out a sob but then felt so angry she suddenly found her voice.

'No!' she shouted, 'Where's Morforwyn. What have you done to her?'

He sniggered.

'She's gone. She fled, just like all the others who come up against the great Malpiddock. She doesn't care about what happens to you anymore.'

'We don't believe you, you're lying!' shouted Bindy. 'You're evil. She wouldn't give up that easily. Her father's innocence is too important to her!'

'Her father's innocence! He'll never come out of that prison alive and she'll be with him if I have my way.' He bent closer to them, so much so, that they both instinctively put out their hands to hold him back.

As they did so they touched his skin and he shrank back suddenly. They both realised at the same time that their touch had an interesting effect on him. Together they walked towards him to touch him again. He went quiet suddenly and backed away.

Feeling a little more confident, Bindy said, 'If you want these jewels you'll have to tell us where Morforwyn is now.'

He looked thoughtful and replied, 'Very well. I'll tell you where she is. Stay where you are.'

He turned and pointed towards a dark corner behind him. As they peered into the shadows, he shot a bright light from his finger into the darkness and they saw the mermaid lying motionless on the floor. She was wrapped in the blanket she'd been weaving and sewing since they'd first met her.

'Her father's burial shroud has come in quite handy,' he said in a sneering manner.

'What have you done to her?' Bindy whispered, horrified at what he might have done.

As Cassie stared at the figure on the ground she suddenly remembered what Morforwyn had said about her mother's accident '. . . . *if he kills her he is guilty of murder and risks his status, his position and his power.*'

'I don't believe she's dead,' she shouted 'Otherwise you'd be guilty of murder. You'd lose all your power.'

He turned towards her and with a fearful rage, rose up to his full height and screamed,

'GIVE ME THE JEWELS NOW!' As the terrible cry filled the cave he suddenly buckled at the waist and fell to the ground. His face held a look of total bewilderment and alarm. He stared at the girls who clung to each other not knowing why he had suddenly dropped to the floor. Then, from behind them came footsteps and a shout,

'Give up, Malpiddock, you are defeated at last.' The figure who spoke the words was beside them. It was Tom. And behind them they felt the comforting arms of Bindy's parents.

Malpiddock's face was contorted in anger and disbelief. He struggled to rise and as he faced the group of humans, he gave a surprised look of recognition as he identified the man who spoke to him. He shook his head in disbelief.

'No . . . . No! Not you!'

'Yes. We meet again, brother.' Cassie, Bindy and her parents blinked hard and stared in amazement at Tom. 'You'll never change, Malpiddock. Your lack of morals was always going to be your downfall, you grasping, self-centred rogue. You always believed that Kullum's success was a travesty but he has something that has completely escaped you, brother, and that is a good and kind heart.'

'Ha! A good heart!' sneered Malpiddock.

'Yes, and a profound honesty and dignity which he carries with him every day throughout the torment you have heaped on him. He was your true friend once, but instead of sharing in his success and supporting him, you've wasted what you could have been and have achieved nothing, except disgrace. Your only friends are greed and power and look where they've got you.'

'Enough!' shouted Malpiddock, 'You're the hypocrite. You helped me!'

'No. You tricked me! I didn't imagine you'd steal from the King and betray Kullum. You can't even be honest with yourself. Face it.' Tom paused and laid down the box which he was still clinging to, its weight giving a dull thud as it hit the floor. He looked again at his brother who was visibly growing weaker and weaker.

'What have you done to me?' Malpiddock demanded. Tom looked down momentarily then looked back at his brother.

'You gave me no alternative. I went to see Dolfo.'

'You're a liar! You said you'd never return.'

'I had no choice, even if it means I have risked my own freedom. I recognised the pain and suffering you were causing to Kullum, Morforwyn, Nesta and these children, just as you did to me. Now he knows everything I know. He has agreed to hold a retrial and these,' he said pointing to the jewels, 'are evidence and will go back with me and Morforwyn to the king, where they belong.'

Malpiddock let out a self-pitying groan realising that King Dolfo must by now have summoned his counsel and had advised them of a retrial. Knowing of Malpiddock's disgrace, this would have lost him their respect and, together with the king's and his brother's disapproval, was having this tremendous affect on his strength. He felt his power ebb away. Tom, noticing he was no longer a threat, sent Mr Hammond out to release the Bartons and to bring them back into the cave.

While they left he attended to Morforwyn. He raised her up and rested her head on his arm. He took out a small box from his pocket and poured its contents onto her face then waited until it took effect. Eventually, she opened her eyes and looked at the man holding her. She tensed and became afraid. The girls rushed over to her.

'It's alright, Morforwyn, it's over. Malpiddock's been stopped and this man has helped us. He's also going to help your father. He's been to see Dolfo and you can both return the jewels to him.'

Tom spoke to Morforwyn in *Miwsong*, the language of the sea, and he calmed her and she understood.

CHAPTER 25

After being happily reunited, both families returned to their cottages to have time to themselves and spent the afternoon reliving the incredible experiences of the day. There were so many questions that were left unanswered but they resigned themselves to never fully understanding everything about their adventures. They were exhausted but happy in the knowledge, at least, that Malpiddock had been defeated at last and that they had been instrumental in helping Morforwyn free her beloved father. It was also their last day in Wales. Thanks to the agents, they'd been able to stay the extra night before going home and to make the most of their last night they had decided to spend a celebratory meal together at the inn in the village.

Mrs Easterson had been released from hospital, surprising all the doctors, who were still scratching their heads as to how she recovered so quickly. The girls left a note at Kittiwake Cottage asking her to join them at seven o'clock.

Once six o'clock came, the ladies and girls made themselves look extra pretty for the night out while the dads waited patiently to get into the bathrooms. Eventually they were ready and they all walked up the lane chatting and laughing. Reaching Kittiwake Cottage, Bindy and Cassie offered to fetch Mrs Easterson so they strolled through the gate and knocked on the door. They heard Mrs Easterson call out,

'Coming!' and soon she opened the door and greeted them with a beaming smile.

'Well my lovely girls, don't you look pretty!'

'You look nice too, Mrs Easterson.' they replied.

'Come on, then, let's go shall we? I don't know about you, but I could do with a nice meal after all that hospital rubbish!'

'Was it that bad?' asked Bindy. Mrs Easterson thought for a moment, looked at them very seriously then replied with complete truthfulness,

'Yes, absolutely dreadful!' They laughed and joined their parents for the walk up to the car park. It was a clear evening with a cool breeze that gently rustled the leaves on the trees.

Meanwhile, in a world far beneath the oceans, King Dolfo was resting inside his cavern when his aid advised that Dabberlock and Morforwyn had arrived. He acknowledged the information with a wave of his hand and summoned them to him.

They entered. Morforwyn held the bag of royal treasures and Dabberlock, grasped the box he had taken control of ever since Bindy and Cassie had discovered it in the garden of Island Cottage.

'Ah,' beamed the king, 'I have been anticipating this moment with much eagerness. I am, forever, indebted to you both' He took the box from Dabberlock and turned the key with a click. Lifting the lid gently he looked down at the imperial crown, which had been skilfully crafted by Dabberlock and Malpiddock's ancestor many generations before. He held it up; it was of the most precious golden metal. Fashioned very much like a bishop's mitre, but with three peaks, it stood tall and straight. Around the base were symbols in many different colours and shapes made from the most beautiful jewels the oceans could produce and above this were carvings of sea creatures; fish, sea horses, corals and merfolk twisting around the body of the crown, their shapes enhanced by different metals and gems from the sea. He replaced it inside its case and closed the lid gently. With a sad shake of his head, he sighed again and looked at Dabberlock.

'What made him do it?'

'Majesty, I have asked myself the same question many times. Malpiddock, even as a young mer-child, became frustrated when things did not always work out the way he wished and instead of learning from them, he would often let the disappointment fester. I believe it reached a climax when Kullum was appointed as your chief magician instead of himself, and, maybe, that was the culmination of all his pent up bitterness. But to come to this . . .' Dabberlock broke off, clearly distressed at what would now happen to his brother, his gifted brother, whom all had admired, especially himself. Even though they had gone their own separate ways years before, there was still a strong brotherly love that he held for Malpiddock.

'Will you return to us now, Dabberlock?' the king asked him.

'I will, of course, have to attend the trial, Majesty, and the council will decide my fate regarding my involvement.

But even if they allow me my freedom, my decision to live a human life has not altered.'

'Can I not change your mind? I have yet to understand what made you chose to leave us. I have often wondered.'

'It was, in the main, my weariness of the constant challenges I faced with Malpiddock. As you know, I am a simple craftsman, Majesty, a simple merman who desires a simple life. Malpiddock being the great, gifted magician couldn't understand that. He constantly nagged at me to improve myself, to give up the work I love and better myself within the imperial court. He always belittled my skills as a rock carver and being my only relative, I sought his approval.

'Then, one day, soon after Kullum was appointed chief magician, he visited my cave and began to admire my work. He asked me to carve ten stones for him, I was delighted. At last he recognised my worth. Then later he asked me to carve out certain shapes from them and fit a lock to them. He flattered me in admiring all I had done and asked me to do more carving. I innocently did this, feeling, at last, approval from my brother.

'Of course, I know now, that he was planning this great deception. When I had completed all the carvings he came to me and told me that I had been very useful and that he would reward me with great wealth in years to come. I told him I didn't want wealth just acknowledgement that I had skills, in the same way he did. He laughed at me. He told me I would always be a fool and that he merely used me for a wrong done to him and that I was now implicated in his plan of revenge. I felt angry and also dejected once more. By using me in that way I confess I became afraid. Although he did not disclose his intentions, I knew what he was capable of and in a cowardly way, perhaps, I vowed to leave the oceans and try my luck on land.' He looked at the king and gave a sad smile. 'I know, now, that I should have tried to dissuade him from whatever he was planning but in my heart I knew he would not tell me his plan or listen to sense. I should have told you too, Majesty, but it was so difficult to betray him.'

The king nodded and looked grave.

'So he planned this, so called, revenge, many years ago. How sad, such a waste.' He turned to Morforwyn and gave her a little smile.

'My dear, come closer.' With a wave of her silvery blue tail she swam to the king's side. He took the bag from her and took her hand in his.

'You are the only one who truly believed your father's innocence. He is a very lucky merman. Please accept my deepest apologies for doubting him. Also, for allowing myself to be persuaded that my trust in him was misguided. He has been my true and trusted servant for many years and I am troubled that I did not believe his innocence.' He bowed his head a little and shook his head, then gazed back at her with a sorrowful look.

'Majesty, please do not be sad. My heart is overflowing with joy and you, also, must feel joy and not sorrow, that the man you always trusted is, and always will be, your true and loyal servant.'

'Yes,' he replied, patting her hand, 'You're absolutely right. Have you had a chance to see him yet?'

'Not yet, Majesty, but as soon as I leave here you won't be able to stop me!' she laughed.

'Tell him I am deeply sorry, Morforwyn, for doubting him.'

'I will, Majesty. '

'Go, now, my dear. Tell him I'll see him soon and, more importantly, my deepest thanks to you, Morforwyn. But wait, I am forgetting. . . .' He took an object from the table next to him. '. . . I want you to accept this royal gift.'

'Oh no, Majesty, no, there is no need.'

'Oh yes, without you the kingdom would be in great danger, so no arguments now . . . .' and with that, he took a precious jewelled tiara, placed it onto her head and with a look of great sincerity added, 'Please accept this with the King's deepest gratitude.' He gave the young mermaid a look of such profound honesty she knew she could not refuse.

CHAPTER 26

When they arrived at the inn, Mrs Easterson and the two families were greeted by a large open fire that roared a cheery welcome. They sat near the bar for some drinks and, after chatting for some time, moved to their table. Throughout the course of their meal they explained to Mrs Easterson everything that had happened to them and their parents. She asked many questions too and all answers were given.

After they had given their orders for desserts, Bindy turned to Mrs Easterson.

'Mrs Easterson, there are some things I still don't understand.'

'What are those, my dear?'

'What do you know about Tom?'

'Nothing at all. I didn't know he was a merman. But then that is usual with merfolk. Once they decide to live a human life they no longer refer to their former lives beneath the sea. It's as if they have been reborn into a new existence, which, in fact, is what it is. I was as surprised as you to learn the truth and as for being Malpiddock's brother! Well, I still can't believe it. They are so different, those two brothers. Tom being so shy and unassuming and that brother of his . . . well, need I say more?'

'That day on the beach, when we were hidden in the dunes and your basket appeared from nowhere, how did it get there?'

'Yes, that was rather good, wasn't it? Well, inside the cave where Morforwyn stayed are tunnels created partly by the sea wearing them away from inside and others which were carved with special instruments that the merfolk have. Underground tunnels mean safety for them and they can travel the length of some beaches. There are some tunnels from her cave which run to parts of the beach including one which happens to end at the rocks close to the base of the sand dunes where you were that day. Morforwyn suggested I use it, so I just chose my moment to climb out, left the basket and then crept back inside the tunnel without you seeing me. You were higher up than I was so you couldn't see me and also you were crouching down and looking the other way, so it wasn't that difficult.'

The waitress brought their desserts and coffee so they resumed their meal for a while. Then Bindy thought of another question,

'Why did you always take your basket to the beach, we noticed it was always empty?'

'Well, I used to take Morforwyn some special tasty snacks and some king prawns to eat, they're her favourite and she couldn't get those in these waters. So I used to take her a little treat.'

'Everything has a simple answer, hasn't it?' said Bindy.

'Yes, usually it does.' replied Mrs Easterson.

'So, who is Nesta then?' asked Cassie.

Everyone looked at her.

'Nesta?' they chorused, looking puzzled.

'Yes, in the cave with Malpiddock, Tom said to him, *'I saw the pain and suffering you were causing to Kullum, Morforwyn, Nesta and these children.'* So who's Nesta?'

Mrs Easterson looked at them all. They were all looking back at her with interest. She smiled and gave a little laugh,

'Well even that has a simple explanation. You see, it's me. I'm Nesta.'

'You!' they all exclaimed.

She nodded. 'I was born Miss Nesta Rose. Rose being my maiden name before I was married. Well, when I wanted to introduce Kullum to my family we realised they'd want to know his surname. Of course, no merman has a surname just a first name, so enjoying word games, he took the letters of my name and made a surname out of them—Easterson, you see? And so when we married we became Mr and Mrs Easterson.'

They all stared at her, each one working out the letters in their heads. She continued, 'Of course there's a bit of irony connected with those word games because when they were young, apparently Kullum and Malpiddock used to enjoy outwitting each other with word puzzles and anagrams and such like and now, of course, we discover that Malpiddock used the jumbled letters of his name to select and steal the special jewels and name the cottages after them.' She stifled a yawn 'Oh dear, excuse me, I must have eaten and drunk too much!'

Mr Hammond said, 'We're all rather tired, I think. We've had an extremely exhausting week.'

'I hope you've managed to enjoy your holiday despite all this frantic adventuring, though.' she said in a rather concerned voice.

They all agreed they'd had a brilliant time. Bindy and Cassie gazed wistfully at each other, both thinking that they wouldn't be seeing each other again. Mrs Barton noticed the look passing between them.

'How would you like to spend some of next year here?' she asked them, looking at the Hammonds with a questioning expression.

'Oh please!' they exclaimed.

'Only if you wash our cars tomorrow morning before we go!' added Mr Barton.

'Oh no, not fair!'

'Only kidding.' He grinned, turning to catch the eye of the waitress for the bill.

The following morning, very early, the girls took a last stroll down to the beach as their parents were packing up their cars and tidying the cottages. Trilby was bounding away across the sand and splashing into the rock pools. They were making plans for next year and promising each other they'd keep in touch and try to meet up before next year. They'd said goodbye to Mrs Easterson and she'd given them a mighty hug each and thanked them once more for all they had done. They were just hoping they could see Morforwyn again and walked towards the rocks to try and call her. Just once more.

At the mouth of the cave they whispered into their shells but after a few minutes of trying they heard nothing. They sat facing the sea looking out at where she might be, just hoping to catch a glimpse as the waves crashed onto the shore. The gulls were calling. They checked their watches and noted that they had to make their way back in ten minutes.

'We mustn't tell anyone, Bindy, you know that don't you.' Cassie said, still looking out to sea.

'I know. I don't want to really. I want it to be our own special secret. Did I tell you, I wanted to go to Disneyland this year? I'm glad I didn't.'

'I'm glad you didn't too.' Cassie flashed her a huge smile.

'And *I'm* extremely glad you didn't.' The girls spun round and there sat Morforwyn just outside her cave looking resplendent. Her face, happy and smiling, her skin glowing and in her hair she wore a tiara of sparkling jewels.

'I'm sorry I took so long to come. I was far away enjoying a celebration which the King was giving in honour of my father. I had to ask his permission to leave and when I told him who was calling he told me to hurry along before I missed you.'

'So everything's alright? Your father's free?'

'Yes, he's free and getting stronger every day. He still has to attend Malpiddock's trial before resuming his duties, but that won't be too long. We are all so grateful to you.'

'We're leaving today.' Cassie advised. 'Can we keep our shells and use them if we come back next year?'

'Of course, I'll wait to hear your call. Before then, however, I have something else for you. She turned and from behind her she brought two gilded boxes about the size of a small shoe box. She handed one each to the girls. The boxes looked very similar to the one found at Island Cottage; the one Tom took control of.

'Look inside.' she urged.

They opened up the boxes and each had compartments for keeping little treasures.

'My own treasure box!' breathed Bindy, 'Oh, Morforwyn, it's beautiful, thank you.'

'Look underneath.' They pulled up the top layer and underneath, the base was lined with mother of pearl. On this lay a beautiful bracelet. It was of the blue metal that had been used to create some of the Royal jewels and from each bracelet hung replicas of the jewels they had rescued interspersed with tiny coloured pearls. They recognised the wonderful mesmerising jewels they had found but also included were the ones they hadn't seen; the frond of deep red coral, the gleaming lobster with jewelled eyes and finally a tiny golden thimble shape. They looked at Morforwyn questioningly.

'Yes, that's what was inside the heavy box, it's a copy of the Imperial Crown.'

'Wow!' they breathed, examining it carefully with its tiny jewels and carvings.

They looked at each one, entranced, the memories flooding back once more as they relived each incredible moment opening the stones.

'They are a gift to you from the king in thanks for returning his jewels and the boxes are from my father and me. I hope you like them.'

'Morforwyn, these are so cool . . . they're *awesome*!' They both rose and hugged her and as they did so, an enchanting tingle seemed to flow through them and they laughed.

THE END

ABOUT THE AUTHOR

Meryl E. Hodgson lives with her husband, daughter, two cats and a dog on the beautiful Gower coast of Swansea, which has been a great source of inspiration for her writing. Originally inspired by her daughter's love of mermaids, this first book grew in answer to a deep need to put pen to paper and create a story that children would love. With humour and an easy style of writing she has captured and created a thrilling atmosphere in this compulsive mystery surrounding those amazing mythical sea creatures which every girl loves.